Oliver Optic

The Starry Flag; or, the Young Fisherman of Cape Ann

Oliver Optic

The Starry Flag; or, the Young Fisherman of Cape Ann

ISBN/EAN: 9783337076948

Printed in Europe, USA, Canada, Australia, Japan

Cover: Foto ©Andreas Hilbeck / pixelio.de

More available books at **www.hansebooks.com**

THE STARRY FLAG;

OR, THE

YOUNG FISHERMAN OF CAPE ANN.

BY

OLIVER OPTIC,

AUTHOR OF "YOUNG AMERICA ABROAD," "THE ARMY AND NAVY STORIES,"
"THE WOODVILLE STORIES," "THE BOAT-CLUB STORIES,"
"THE RIVERDALE STORIES," ETC.

BOSTON:
LEE AND SHEPARD.
1868.

TO

M<small>Y</small> Y<small>OUNG</small> F<small>RIEND</small>,

JANE LEE TAYLOR,

𝔗𝔥𝔦𝔰 𝔅𝔬𝔬𝔨

IS AFFECTIONATELY DEDICATED.

THE STARRY FLAG SERIES,

BY OLIVER OPTIC.

TO BE COMPLETED IN SIX VOLUMES.

I. THE STARRY FLAG; OR, THE YOUNG FISHERMAN OF CAPE ANN.

II. BREAKING AWAY; OR, THE FORTUNES OF A STUDENT.

III. SEEK AND FIND; OR, THE ADVENTURES OF A SMART BOY.

Others in preparation.

PREFACE.

THE STARRY FLAG is the first of a series of stories now in course of publication in "Oliver Optic's Magazine, OUR BOYS AND GIRLS." As it appeared in weekly instalments, it was received with a degree of favor as unexpected as it was gratifying to the author; and he gratefully acknowledges the kindness of his young friends, whose partiality to his works has been so often and so agreeably manifested.

Although this story is mainly fiction, it is not without a foundation of truth, both in the relations of the hero to his uncle, and in the singular event upon which the turning-point of the plot rests. The localities of the various incidents are intended to be correctly described, as they were fixed in the mind of the writer by a pleasant sojourn of a few weeks on Cape Ann during a summer vacation.

It is more important that the hero should be worthy of the admiration and regard of the reader than that merely local

(5)

surroundings should be accurately delineated; and the author hopes that his young friends, while they strive to be as resolute and daring as Levi, will also endeavor to be as noble and true, as void of offence before God and man, as he labored to be.

Since the publication of The Starry Flag was completed in the Magazine, the author has found allusions to it in at least a hundred letters from young persons, who seem to be strongly impressed with the opinion that the *whole* story has not been told. Though it was not his original purpose to write a second story with the same characters, the author has neither the inclination nor the courage to disappoint his young friends, and at no distant period the fortunes of Levi Fairfield and Bessie Watson will be followed to a more satisfactory conclusion in a Sequel to The Starry Flag.

HARRISON SQUARE, MASS.,
September 17, 1867.

CONTENTS.

CHAPTER I.

THE DINGY DORY. 11

CHAPTER II.

TWO HUNDRED AND FIFTY DOLLARS. 22

CHAPTER III.

DOCK VINCENT. 33

CHAPTER IV.

A PITCHED BATTLE. 45

CHAPTER V.

LEVI FAIRFIELD'S CHAMBER. 57

CHAPTER VI.

WHO STOLE THE WALLET ? 69

CHAPTER VII.

OFF EASTERN POINT. 80

8   CONTENTS.

CHAPTER VIII.

THE TEMPEST AND THE WRECK. 92

CHAPTER IX.

AFTER THE SQUALL. 102

CHAPTER X.

DOCK VINCENT'S LITTLE PLAN. 114

CHAPTER XI.

LEVI'S CHAMBER. 126

CHAPTER XII.

LEVI MAKES A SPEECH. 137

CHAPTER XIII.

MR. HATCH'S TESTIMONY. 149

CHAPTER XIV.

AFTER THE EXAMINATION. 161

CHAPTER XV.

LEVI EXPLORES THE CHIMNEY. 172

CHAPTER XVI.

ON MIKE'S POINT. 183

CHAPTER XVII.

THE EVIL MAN. 194

CHAPTER XVIII.

The Starry Flag goes to Sea. 205

CHAPTER XIX.

Dock Vincent's Letter. 216

CHAPTER XX.

The Cruise of the Starry Flag. 228

CHAPTER XXI.

The Starry Flag comes to Anchor. . . . 239

CHAPTER XXII.

Homeward Bound. 251

CHAPTER XXIII.

The Night and the Gale. 263

CHAPTER XXIV.

The Return of the Starry Flag. 274

CHAPTER XXV.

The Result of the Examination. 286

CHAPTER XXVI.

Conclusion. 300

THE STARRY FLAG;

OR,

THE YOUNG FISHERMAN OF CAPE ANN.

CHAPTER I.

THE DINGY DORY.

BUT I must have one more bath before we go father," said Bessie Watson, as she gazed down into the clear, blue waters of the sea, which surged against the rocks near the hotel on Cape Ann, where she and her parents had been spending a week.

"There is hardly time, Bessie," replied Mr. Watson, as he consulted his watch.

"What time is it, father?"

"Quarter past eight."

"There is time enough then."

"I don't like to have you bathe here, Bessie. It

is a dangerous place, and I'm going to Rye Beach almost wholly because you are so fond of the salt water. I have been afraid, every time you went in, that you would slip off that rock."

" There is no danger."

" I think there is."

" The rope will prevent any accident."

" The rope is some protection, but I don't think the place is safe."

" Just one more plunge, pa; I shall feel so much better for the journey!" pleaded Bessie, whose bright eyes and pretty face were so eloquent that the indulgent father could not resist them.

Undoubtedly Mr. Watson was entirely correct in his estimate of the bathing facilities of the particular point on Cape Ann of which we write. The hotel was located on high land, which terminated at the shore in ragged rocks and steep precipices. There was no beach, not even a patch of sand, on which the bather could obtain a foothold. A sloping rock, which afforded not more than a couple of square rods of flat surface, had been selected for bathing purposes. A rope, secured on perpendicular iron bars set in the rock, had been stretched around it, to prevent the bathers from being carried off by the surf, or from venturing beyond their depth.

Mr. Watson was a wealthy merchant from the city, and Bessie was his only child. If she had not been spoiled by over-indulgence, it was because there was so little waywardness in her nature; because she was too gentle and affectionate to take advantage of the weakness of her parents. Bathing in itself was a pleasant and harmless recreation; and, as it was the principal élement of sea-shore life, Bessie thought it was quite proper that she should indulge in a plunge on the present occasion. There was no possible objection except the alleged insecurity of the place; and, as she had bathed there a half a dozen times before without being washed off the rocks, it might be done just once more.

Her father yielded the point; and it was a happy reflection for him that this was the last time he should be compelled to yield. The bathing dresses were sent for, and father and daughter made haste to improve the short time left to them for the invigorating recreation. During the night the wind had

2

been blowing fresh from the south-west, which in this locality always produces a heavy sea. The weather was now warm and pleasant, with a light breeze from the westward; but the waves, from the effects of the night wind, were still strong and heavy.

Bessie rushed into the water, closely followed by her father. A great billow immediately "tipped her over;" but she sprang to her feet again, leaping and shouting with childish delight. It was rare sport to her; and, if she had been a fish, to the watery "manor born," she could not have enjoyed it more, nor have felt more perfectly at home. Another great wave rolled up, and again she was lifted from her feet like a piece of cork, and would have been dashed against the bathing hut, if she had not grasped the rope.

"This won't do, Bessie," said Mr. Watson, shaking his head.

"Why, pa, I think it's delicious," replied Bessie, in a silvery scream.

"The waves are a great deal stronger than I supposed. I can hardly keep my feet."

"O, do keep them, pa! You will want them when we get to Rye," shouted the excited little miss.

" Come, Bessie, don't stay in any longer."

" We haven't been·in two minutes. Don't go out yet, — that's a dear pa."

" I'm afraid the sea will carry you off. Be a good girl, Bessie, and go out now."

" Just a minute or two longer, father. I will keep hold of the rope; I won't let go; and I shall be just as safe here as I should be in the house."

" Be very careful then, for you have no idea of the strength of these waves."

" There isn't a bit of danger, pa — not a bit," replied the sylph, as she extended her agile form upon the water, and began to beat the blue brine with her delicate little feet.

But the water was not quite deep enough near the cliff for certain aquatic feats, suggested to her vivid imagination by the presence of the rope, and she followed the line out to the part which ran parallel with the shore. There she hung under the guard, and flapped and floundered, and kicked and buffeted the great waves, screaming all the time, as young ladies always do, in the exuberance of her delight. Her father attempted to assist her in the

exhilarating fun of the occasion ; but he was so anxious and so nervous for the safety of the sportive
little mermaid, that he did not materially increase
the merriment of the moment, though his presence
was always a joy to his daughter.

About the time Bessie's tiny feet touched the cooling waters, a dory, loaded to the rail, and heaped up
in the middle, with dog-fish, rounded the rocky point,
a few rods beyond the bathing-place. This boat contained the hero of our story, and it was quite proper
that it should round the point at this particular moment, when our readers are reasonably sure that Miss
Bessie will unfortunately lose her hold of the guard
rope, and be carried out into the deep water by a
treacherous retreating wave.

The dory which contained the important personage
alluded to, whose presence suggests heroic deeds and
tender words, was not at all like Cleopatra's barge,
and was utterly unworthy the honor of receiving on
board the gentle water-sprite who was laving her
locks in the brine on the ledge. The dory had been
pieced and patched till there was not much of the
original fabric left. She had been tinned and tin-

kered, tarred and pitched, calked and puttied, until
she would condescend to remain on the top of the
water, apparently in acknowledgment of the perseverance rather than the skill of him who had the
audacity to attempt to make such a craft float. But
she did float, and bore up a goodly freight of staring
dog-fish.

Bent on a rude mast, stepped through the fore
thwart of the dory, was a small sprit-sail, which, like
the hull beneath it, was " a thing of shreds and
patches," and which was even a better exponent of
the ingenuity and perseverance of him who spread it
to the breeze of that soft summer morning. Nearly
amidships, with the dog-fish heaped up before and
behind him, sat the author and finisher — more especially the finisher — of the dingy, uncouth, and un-
graceful craft we have described. With both hands
he held a worm-eaten oar firmly against the side of
the boat, the blade projecting down into the water
below the bottom of the dory, thus serving the
double purpose of keel and rudder.

Levi Fairfield would not have passed muster in
the drawing-room of wealth and fashion, or even in

the humbler parlor of the Cape Ann nabob; but he
was an exceedingly good fellow for all that, and fit
to be the hero of a more pretentious story than the
one we aspire to tell.   It is quite true that his
clothes consisted of as many patches as his sail, and
as mighty a struggle had been made to induce them
to hold together, as had been expended on the boat
itself; and they were daubed from head to foot with
dog-fish slime, to say nothing of numerous dabs of
paint and pitch, tar and grease.   But underneath this
garb of unseemly cut and doubtful unity were iron
muscles and a heart of steel.   Inconsistent as it was
with his homely dress, and inconsistent as it may
seem to present a youthful hero in the first chapter
with his wealth already piled up, Levi Fairfield's fortune — as fortunes were measured on Cape Ann —
was made.   His father had left him considerable
property, and his uncle, whose only god was money,
had been appointed his guardian.

Levi was ambitious, not for his future alone, but
for the present.   There were two things he wanted,
and of which he felt himself to be especially in
need — a new suit of clothes and a new boat; and

he wanted the boat more than he wanted the clothes, — which will not seem very strange to all wide-awake boys, fond of snuffing salt-water air, and sailing in crack boats.

On the week before we present our aquatic hero to the reader, there had been a great fair held in a mammoth tent by one of the religious societies in the place, to obtain money to build a church. A devout and devoted brother in a neighboring town had built a sail-boat, a handsome and substantial craft, and presented it to the church, to be sold for the benefit of the enterprise. This boat, patriotically named "The Starry Flag," had been sent round to the town, and moored at a wharf near the great tent. It had been used to carry out parties from the fair, and thus contributed something to the object; but it had not been sold.

"The Starry Flag" was Levi's ideal of a good boat, and he used to gaze at her with delighted eyes from his dilapidated dory. He longed to possess her; longed to own her; to go a-fishing and sailing in her. Not alone as a pleasure craft did he covet her; but he felt that he could make her pay. What a load of dog-fish she could bring in! What a party of ladies and gentlemen he could take out to the fishing grounds in her! In a word, she would be a present fortune to him.

He entertained some serious thoughts of applying to his uncle for two hundred and fifty dollars, the sum asked for " The Starry Flag ; " but he rejected the idea after faithful consideration, for he knew that it would be easier to squeeze a quart of milk out of a cubic foot of Rockport granite, than to get two hundred and fifty dollars out of his uncle for any purpose whatever, — unless it was to pay his nephew's funeral expenses. Levi wanted that boat, and he continued to want it up to the time when he rounded the point beyond the bathing-place.

We assure our impatient readers who have consented to follow us through this account of Levi Fairfield and his antecedents, that Bessie Watson is not yet drowned, and hasn't even slipped off the flat rock into the deep water. We regret the delay, but it would be absurd to have a young lady rescued from a watery grave without knowing anything about the person who is to achieve the heroic deed. In the next, if not in the present generation, when a bold-hearted young fellow is to rescue a helpless damsel from impending fire or water, it will be absolutely necessary to introduce him before he plunges in.

After leading our readers to anticipate the appalling event suggested at the beginning of this chapter, it would be cruel to disappoint them; and, with no ill-will against poor Bessie, whom we both admire and love, we are compelled to let her lose her hold upon the rope, and to permit the ugly wave, with one fell swoop, to bear her far out beyond the reach of her agonized father.

"See me, pa!" shouted she, as she sprang out of the water into the air, just as the "tenth wave," the greatest of all, swept under her. "Isn't this fun!"

She descended as the billow rolled back whitened with foam from the rocks, and buried herself in the milky surge. The heavy volume of water rushed against her, wrenched her grasp from the line, and carried her shrieking out into the water.

CHAPTER II.

TWO HUNDRED AND FIFTY DOLLARS.

LEVI FAIRFIELD was fifteen years old when his dingy dory rounded the point above where Bessie Watson was bathing. His father had been a fisherman, and had made a Cape Ann fortune in the fishing business. It is rather beneath the dignity of history, and even of the higher flights of story-telling, to descend to particulars; but we are compelled, in this instance, to acknowledge that Captain Fairfield's fortune was only fifteen thousand dollars, as rated by the appraisers after his decease; and even these figures shrank to ten thousand when the smacks were sold, and the debts due his estate collected.

This was Levi Fairfield's fortune, and there was not the least need for him to soil his trousers with dabs of tar and rancid grease. When Captain Fairfield was dead, as Levi, then only eight years old,

had no mother, the probate court, in its ineffable
wisdom, appointed the lad's uncle to be the guardian
of his person and his property — to feed, clothe, and
educate him in a manner conforming to his worldly
circumstances. The selection would have been a very
good one, if Nathan Fairfield, the captain's brother,
had been a decent man, with even tolerably enlarged
ideas of the duty a parent or guardian owes to a
child, especially when the child has money to pay for
all he needs — moral, intellectual, and material.

Uncle Nathan was mean, close, parsimonious — he
called it economical. He sent the boy to school two
months in the winter, and worked him like a truck-
horse the rest of the time. It was generally believed
that, if Levi should fall overboard and be drowned,
or tumble off a cliff and break his neck, his guardian
would not mourn as one without hope.

When Levi attained the age of fourteen, he began
to have some decided views of his own. He liked
to work, but he wanted to make something by his
labor. He felt the need of a little more learning
than his uncle's stingy policy had permitted him to
obtain. Having a will of his own, he had already

decided to purchase a fine schooner, and go into the
fishing business as soon as the law would allow him
to handle his own money. He was a boy of energy
and enterprise, and in spite of his uncle, who had no
claim upon his time, he had already gone to work on
his own hook, mainly for the purpose of improving
his education. Purchasing the wreck of an old dory
with money earned by himself, he had made it into
the craft in which we now find him.

Levi was dissatisfied with his position. He was
worth ten thousand dollars, and dressed meaner than
the sons of fishermen and stone-cutters. He had
another suit of clothes at home, but it was hardly
better than that he wore; at least, it was none too
good to wear every day; but uncle Nathan held the
purse-strings, and would not loosen them while the
rags held together. There was a very wide difference of opinion between them on this subject, as
indeed there was on many others, so that their relations were far from harmonious and agreeable.

As Levi sat in the dory, proud and happy in the
possession of so many dog-fish, whose unctuous livers
would add eight or ten dollars to his worldly wealth,

he glanced occasionally at the beautiful little sylph who was beating the angry waves with her delicate limbs. He had seen Bessie Watson before, and it had even occurred to him that she was the fairest young lady he had ever beheld.

"Creation!" shouted the young fisherman, as he saw the receding wave tear her from the rope, and bear her far out from her father.

"Help me! O, help me!" cried the little maiden, terribly alarmed, as the great waves lifted her on their stormy crests, and then buried her beneath the surges.

Her father was filled with agony. He was no swimmer, but he fearlessly plunged from the rope, and attempted to reach his struggling child. He was powerless to save her, for he could not even save himself.

Levi Fairfield let out the sheet of his ragged sail, and headed the dory, which was jumping wildly over the waves, towards the spot where Bessie was struggling for life. He was a skilful boatman, and, putting his helm down, he "spilled" the sail, and came to at the leeward of her. Reaching out, he grasped

3

Bessie by the arm, and attempted to pull her into the boat ; but the dory was loaded to its utmost capacity, and refused to be further imposed upon, even in so good a cause. In spite of Levi's care and skill, the dory rolled over, and emptied a large portion of the dog-fish into the sea. But the intrepid youth held on to his fair burden, and, taking to the water himself, finally succeeded in getting her into the dory.

By this time the young fisherman was completely exhausted by his exertions, and could only hold on at the gunwale of the water-logged craft. A boat had already put off from the shore, and having rescued Mr. Watson, came to the assistance of Levi.

"O father ! father !" cried Bessie, as she sprang into his arms, "I am safe."

"My child !" exclaimed the father, whose eyes were involuntarily raised to heaven as he clasped her to his heart, in devout thanksgiving for the safety of the beloved child.

"I've lost nearly all my dog-fish," said Levi, as he climbed over the stern of the dory.

- The boatman who had picked up Mr. Watson

pulled to the shore with his passengers, paying no
attention to the situation of the young fisherman.
Levi needed no assistance. Hauling up his sheet, he
filled away again, and soon reached the shore. The
adventure, however romantic, was not entirely satisfactory to the fisherman, for he had lost two thirds
of his cargo, and neither father nor daughter had yet
even thanked him for his services.

It is of no use to cry for spilled milk, or spilled
dog-fish; therefore Levi did not cry. He threw the
remainder of his fish into a hollow in the rocks, and
baled out the dory, intending to pull out and save
what he could of those which had gone overboard.
While he was thus occupied, Mr. Watson and Bessie,
who had dried and dressed themselves in the bathing
hut, and were hardly the worse for the catastrophe,
approached the spot.

"Young man, you have saved my daughter's life,
and I am very grateful to you," said Mr. Watson.

"O, that's nothing, sir. I always pick up anything
I find adrift," replied Levi, with a broad laugh.

"You saved me, and I shall remember you as
long as I live," added Bessie, warmly.

Both father and daughter expressed their admiration and gratitude for the prompt and skilful manner in which he had rescued the little maiden from the waves.

"Now, Levi, what can I do for you? I owe you more than I can ever pay."

"I don't charge anything, sir, for what I've done. I should expect to be picked up myself if I broke adrift, as the young lady did, and I'm always willing to do as much as that for any one," replied Levi. "I'm sure I would like to save a nice girl like her every day in the week."

Levi cast a timid glance of admiration at Bessie, and her father seemed to have some doubts about offering to pay one with so much pride and dignity for what he had done.

"I shall gratefully remember you as long as I live; but I wish to do something for you now," added the merchant.

"I don't ask anything; but if you have a mind to pay for the dog-fish I lost overboard in the scrape, I will call it square."

"How much are they worth?" laughed Mr. Watson.

"Well, I don't know — five or six dollars. That will make me whole, and I don't want anything more."

"I will certainly do that; and I wish to do much more. Is this your boat?" asked the merchant, pointing to the dingy dory.

"Yes, sir; such as she is, she is mine."

"It isn't much of a boat."

"That's a fact. But she's the best I can get. I fixed her up, so she answers pretty well."

"Don't you want a better boat?"

"I expect to have one some time."

"Wouldn't you like one now?"

"I don't know but I would."

"Do you know of a good one about here?"

"There was one round here — 'The Starry Flag;' may be you have seen her. She's a nice boat, if you want one."

"Where is she now?"

"They have taken her round to Gloucester."

"What is the price of her?"

"Two hundred and fifty dollars."

"Do you know where to find her?"

3 *

"I think I could find her."

"You shall have her, Levi."

"I!" exclaimed the young fisherman. "I gave her up some time ago."

"I will make you a present of her," added Mr. Watson.

"Well, no, sir; I don't exactly like that way of doing things," replied Levi, gazing upon the rock at his feet, sorely tempted by the offer, yet disliking to be paid for the humane act he had done.

"You need a better boat, Levi, and I insist upon your having The Starry Flag."

"I don't want to be paid."

"I'm not going to pay you, my boy: I couldn't do that, if I tried. I am going to Rye to-day, but I will give you the money to pay for the boat, and you shall go to Gloucester for her yourself."

"I want the boat very bad, I won't deny; and perhaps I'll borrow the money of you. I'm rich myself, but my stingy uncle won't give me a red cent."

"You need not borrow it," said the merchant, taking two hundred and fifty dollars from his pocket. "It is yours."

"On the whole, I guess I will borrow it," replied Levi, taking the bills. "I don't want anything for saving your daughter."

"Let him borrow it, father, if he wants to," interposed Bessie, who was delighted with Levi's honesty and delicacy.

Mr. Watson yielded the point, though it is not at all likely that he intended the money should ever be returned to him.

"And here is ten dollars for the fish you lost," added the merchant, handing him another bill.

"It's only six dollars at the most, and I can't change this," replied Levi.

"Never mind ; take the whole of it."

"There comes the stage, father ; we must hurry up to the house," said Bessie.

"Good by, Levi," added Mr. Watson. "I shall never forget you, and I mean to do something more for you."

"Stop a minute ; I want to give you my note for this money, and get your change."

"I can't stop now," laughed the rich merchant. "Come, Bessie."

"Good by, Levi," said the water sprite, giving him her little hand. "I shall always remember you and pray for you."

"Thank you, miss; it's not every fellow that gets a chance to pick up a lady like you in the water. Good by."

She bounded after her father, leaving Levi with two hundred and sixty dollars in his hand. He was astonished and delighted at the result of the adventure.

"The Starry Flag is mine as sure as I'm alive!" exclaimed he, as Mr. Watson and Bessie disappeared beyond the cliff.

CHAPTER III.

DOCK VINCENT.

TWO hundred and fifty dollars!" exclaimed Levi Fairfield, as he looked at the bills in his hand. " I wouldn't have believed it; but it's a fact. I rather think uncle Nathan's eyes would stick out some, if he saw these big figures. But they are not for him to see; he'd take the money away from me, and make me dress in rags, as he always has."

Levi rolled up the bills, and placed them in a dilapidated wallet he carried in his pocket. The bright vision of "The Starry Flag" was actually realized; or it would be, if his miserly uncle did not get the money away from him. With the new boat he could make money enough to procure all the clothes he needed, and to buy a whole library of books. He intended to go to school for six months, as soon as the boating season was over, whether his uncle was willing or not. He was fond of reading, and so far as his time and means would permit, he indulged the taste.

It was necessary that he should conceal the two hundred and fifty dollars from his uncle, until the new boat had been purchased. He had taken it as a loan from Mr. Watson, and he intended to pay it when he came into possession of his property. He chose to take this view of his acceptance of the money, for it was pleasanter than the idea of being paid for doing a deed of kindness. He wished to go immediately to Gloucester, and buy the boat; but he could not go in the ragged and filthy garments he wore, now drenched with water, and it would excite the curiosity of his uncle and aunt if he went home and changed them. He hoped that at dinner time he should be able to effect his purpose.

As there was nothing to be done about the business at present, he sat down in the sun, which was rapidly drying his wet clothes, and proceeded to extract the livers from the dog-fish. He had been unusually fortunate this morning. It was his third trip of the season, and he was satisfied, before he lost any of his fish, that the cargo would yield him about ten dollars' worth of livers, which were then selling at a dollar and a half a bucket. With the ten dollars Mr. Watson had given him, the proceeds of the trip would amount to at least thirteen dollars, which, with what he had before, increased his funds to twenty-one dollars.

Levi felt like a rich man, independent of the two hundred and fifty dollars, which he regarded as a loan ; and he was determined, when he went to Gloucester for The Starry Flag, to buy a suit of clothes. He had enough to think of, therefore, and was so busy that he did not notice the approach of a man, who was descending the rocks to the place where he sat.

" Well, Levi, you lost most of your dog-fish in that scrape," said Dock Vincent, the person who had gone out in the boat after Mr. Watson and his daughter, when he reached the place where the young fisherman was at work.

" I lost a good many of them," replied Levi, rather coldly, for Dock Vincent was not a person whom he regarded with much favor.

"What did he give you?"

"He did the handsome thing by me."

"Did he!" sneered Dock. "He is the meanest man this side of Cape Horn."

"I don't think so," added Levi, decidedly.

"What do you think he gave me for saving his life?" demanded Dock.

"I don't know. I didn't ask anything for what I did. Besides, he had got hold of the rope before you reached him."

"I don't care if he had; I like to see a man who has plenty of money, as he has, show something like gratitude when a fellow does him a good turn."

"Didn't he thank you?"

"Thank me? O, yes. He talked well enough — he and his daughter both; but I wish I had left him where I found him."

"He wouldn't have been drowned if you had."

"I don't know about that," said Dock, shaking his head.

"Didn't he give you anything?" asked Levi, who was much surprised to hear Mr. Watson charged with meanness.

"Yes, he gave me something," answered Dock, with a shrug of the shoulders. "He gave me a hundred-dollar bill."

"Well, I think that's a pretty good day's work for you."

"He ought to have given me a thousand; and if he had given me five thousand it wouldn't have hurt him."

"I think a hundred was very handsome. You only pulled out a few rods from the shore, and were not gone fifteen minutes."

"That's nothing to do with it; he was mean, and he shall pay for it yet. I'll make it cost him twenty thousand dollars."

"What do you mean, Dock?" exclaimed Levi, suspending his work, and looking up into the sinister face of his companion.

"I mean something, Levi," replied Dock, with a mysterious look. "What did he give you?"

"He paid me ten dollars for the dog-fish I lost," answered the young fisherman, evasively.

"Ten dollars! Why, you saved the girl's life, if I didn't her father's. She would have gone down,

4

as sure as the world, before I could have reached
her. Ten dollars! That was meaner than dirt."

"Well, he did the handsome thing by me," added
Levi, unwilling that Mr. Watson should suffer even
for a single day in the estimation of his companion,
though it was not prudent for him to say that he
was the happy possessor of two hundred and fifty
dollars until the boat had been purchased. "I'll tell
you to-morrow just what he did."

"Did he give you a thousand dollars, Levi?"

"No, he did not, nor anything like it."

"Then he was mean. Levi, if you want to make
a heap of money, I will put you in the way of doing
it," said Dock, in a low . 3.

"How?"

"Will you keep still about it?"

"I don't know whether I will or not. On the
whole, I guess I won't have anything to do with it,"
answered Levi, who was quite sure that any of
Dock's schemes for making "a heap of money"
could not be very honest.

"If a hundred dollars was enough for me, he ought
to have given you a thousand."

"I don't think so."

"I do, and everybody will say so. Don't you want to go round to Gloucester with me after dinner?" continued Dock, in the most insinuating of tones. "I'm going round in my schooner, and we can talk over this matter on the way."

"What matter?"

"About the money."

"I don't want to talk about it; I am satisfied now; and if you want to ask Mr. Watson for any more money, you must do it without me."

"You don't understand me, Levi."

"I don't want to understand you, if you are going to do any such dirty work as that. I felt mean to take anything; and I would cut my right hand off before I would ask for more."

"Will you go round with me, Levi?"

The young fisherman wanted to go to Gloucester, but he did not wish to have anything to do with Dock Vincent, who was a reckless, dissipated, and dishonest man. He was the owner of a schooner of seventy tons, in which he carried freights from Rockport and Gloucester to Boston. It was plain that

Dock — his full name was Waldock Vincent — had
a purpose in his mind, in whose execution he was
anxious to have Levi join him, and which he wished
to discuss with him on the passage to the neighboring port.

The young fisherman had no suspicion that his
purpose was anything worse than to ask Mr. Watson
for one or two thousand dollars as a reward for their
services in rescuing the father and daughter. Dock
kept his own counsel, and did not hint at his real
intentions, not doubting that one who had been so
well abused by his uncle was ripe for any scheme,
even if it involved some risk. What Levi regarded
as Dock's intention was bad enough, and the brave
boy — morally brave now — finally refused even to
visit Gloucester with the dangerous man.

"I'm going to ask him to do what is right," added
Dock.

"Ask him for yourself, then, not for me. To-morrow, if I see you, I will tell you what he gave me."

"Well, I want to - see you to-morrow about this
matter. I think you'll come to it, after you have
thought it over."

"No, I shall not."

Dock went off at last, satisfied that nothing could be done with Levi at present.

"Ask him for more money! Humph! I wouldn't do it if I was sure he would give me a million dollars," said Levi to himself. "I should as soon think of asking uncle Nathan for a thousand dollars as Mr. Watson for another hundred. I'm rich now."

Levi finished his work, and carried the livers he had obtained to a man in the vicinity who bought them, and having received the money for them, he went home to dinner. The house of Nathan Fairfield was a type of the man. It was an unpainted, dingy, dilapidated building, with tumble-down sheds and broken fences. Within it was cheerless and uncomfortable. The owner never spent a dollar when by any expedient it could be saved. His wife was sharp and close, like himself. They were well mated, and either of them would grumble all day over the loss or the misuse of a three-cent piece.

The intelligence of the exciting event off the cliff had been thoroughly circulated in the neighborhood,

4 *

and Levi's uncle and aunt were already informed that
he had saved the life of Bessie Watson. Dock Vincent, for his own purposes, had declared that Levi
had received only ten dollars for his services; but
even this sum was enough to excite the cupidity of
his uncle. His guardian questioned him in regard to
the affair, and Levi gave a truthful account of the
rescue of the father and daughter.

"How much did he give you?" asked his uncle.

"He *gave* me ten dollars for the fish I lost," replied Levi, still deeming the larger sum a loan.

"You've been selling livers too — haven't you?"

"Yes, sir — I have."

"How many have you sold?"

"All I could get," replied Levi, who was not disposed to talk very freely on this subject.

"Answer me!" said uncle Nathan sternly. "How
much money have you got now?"

"Twenty-one dollars," replied Levi, desperately.

"Twenty-one dollars!" exclaimed the miser, open-
ing his eyes with astonishment. "That's a great
deal of money for a boy to have. I think you had
better give it to me."

"I don't think I had. I want it to buy some clothes," said Levi, firmly.

"You don't need any clothes. I want you to give me that money."

"I don't want to give it to you; I want it myself."

"Levi, I'm your guardeen, and you must give me that money."

"No, sir, I shall not, guardeen or no guardeen."

"Accordin to law, that money belongs to me to take care on," said uncle Nathan, angrily.

"You take too good care of it for me. You are my guardian, but you keep me short, and make me go ragged. I earned this money myself, and I'm going to get some clothes with it."

"No, you are not. I'm not goin to let you have twenty-one dollars to fool away. · Give it to me, this minute."

"I'm willing to do anything that's right," replied Levi, warmly, "but when you get this money, the chickens will all be old hens."

"Will you give it to me, or shall I take it from you?" demanded the uncle, fiercely, as he stepped towards the boy.

"Neither," answered Levi, retreating to the window.

"You young villain, I'll teach you what a guardeen is."

Uncle Nathan, roused to the highest pitch of anger, rushed forward, and seized Levi by the collar.

CHAPTER IV.

A PITCHED BATTLE.

L EVI was alarmed for the two hundred and fifty dollars in his pocket. He knew that if his uncle once got his hand upon the money, it would be as impossible to remove it as it would be to roll back the tide of the sea. Besides, uncle Nathan had a talent for getting his hands into other people's pockets, at least in a figurative sense; and in the present instance the act threatened to be altogether too literal for the safety of Levi's high-wrought visions of owning and sailing The Starry Flag. He was quite willing to concede his uncle's legal right to the care of all his money; but there was something wrong, and, being no lawyer, he couldn't tell exactly what it was.

Uncle Nathan was so mean and stingy that he was hated and despised by all his neighbors and

acquaintances; and there were plenty of people to
say that it was a shame for a boy to be brought up
as his nephew was. The boy was deprived of proper
food, clothing, and education. His home was the
most disagreeable place he visited within the twenty-
four hours of a day; and Levi, looking at the pleasant dwellings, the happy homes, of other people, could
not help feeling that his lot was hard, and that the
sons of even the common laborers were better off
than he was.

Smarting under the general sense of wrong, Levi
felt that it was his duty to do something to better
his condition. Boldly and bravely he was doing it.
He was working like a common laborer for the com-
forts of life, which his uncle meanly denied him.
And now, to have the fruits of his toil wrested from
him by the same hard hand which had all along
robbed him of suitable food and raiment — for which
his father's estate was charged — was intolerable to
him. It was worth a hard fight, in his estimation, to
save even the twenty-one dollars, and much more to
save the two hundred and fifty, with which he was
to purchase The Starry Flag.

He was roused to the highest pitch of anger and resentment. It was bad enough to·eat such a dinner as that set before him, and to dress in rags; but to have his own money, that for which he had worked hard, taken from him, roused his indignation to such a degree that he was ready to be torn in pieces rather than yield. It might be law for his uncle to take his money, but under the circumstances he felt that it would not be justice.

"Give me that money!" said uncle Nathan, savagely, as he tightened his grasp upon Levi's collar.

"Le' me alone," cried Levi, struggling to escape.

"I'll let you alone when you give me the money."

"I won't give you the money! I'll die first!" replied Levi, giving a desperate spring towards the middle of the room.

Uncle Nathan was a powerful man, and when there was any money concerned he always held on tight. Holding the young man by the collar, he attempted to thrust his hand into the pocket wherein had been deposited the dilapidated wallet.

"Le' me be!" shouted Levi.

"My sakes!" exclaimed Mrs. Fairfield; "the boy's
getting worse every year."

Levi doubled himself up in such a way as to prevent his uncle from reaching his pocket.

"Here, wife, you hold his hands," said the guardian, puffing under the violence of his exertions.

"Sakes alive! I dassn't tech him," replied the
matron, timidly approaching the combatants.

"Go behind him, and get hold of his arms," added
uncle Nathan.

To avoid being flanked in this manner, Levi backed
up towards the table. Uncle Nathan attempted to
pull him away, so as to afford his timid but willing
ally, a chance to assist him. The boy felt that the
battle was going against him, and it was necessary
for him to make a final onslaught. He kicked, strug-
gled, and twisted. He jumped up, lay down, and in
some measure exhausted his persecutor, who had
relaxed his exertions, though he still held on like a
bull-dog. Levi was young and active, and though
his breath was nearly gone, he declined to suspend
the struggle.

The resolute youth had been backed up against the

A PITCHED BATTLE. Page 49.

table again, where his exhausted oppressor wished *
to hold him for a moment, while he recovered his
breath. As this seemed to be the. moment for final
action, Levi renewed his efforts with redoubled energy.
His back was against the table, and in his desperate
effort to release himself, he had doubled himself up
under the extended leaf. Like everything else in
the mansion of Nathan Fairfield, this piece of furniture was a worn-out and rickety concern; and as
Levi sprang up, he carried the leaf up with him,
upsetting the table, and causing all the dishes to
slide off upon the floor.

A general crash ensued; ruin and destruction
among the dishes followed, which so astonished and
confounded uncle Nathan, that he loosed his hold
upon the little monster, and gazed with horror upon
the wreck, from which Levi extricated himself with
all possible haste. Mrs. Fairfield held up both of
her bony hands in grief and terror, as she gazed
upon the broken plates and bowls. The dishes were
old and black, were "nicked" and cracked in every
direction. They were of different colors, sizes, and
shapes; but they were property, and such a terrible

5

devastation filled the miser and his wife with consternation and sorrow. They gazed upon the wreck in real anguish, as though a dear friend had been struck dead before their eyes.

"There! see what you've done!" gasped uncle Nathan, when his horror and his want of breath would permit him to speak.

"I didn't do it; you did it yourself," replied Levi, retreating towards the back door, so as not to be flanked again.

"You didn't do it, you whelp!" said the guardian, angrily, as he stepped towards the panting youth.

"No, I didn't; you did it yourself."

"You must be taken care of, Levi."

"I'd like to be taken care of better than I ever was yet; but as you won't take care of me, I'm going to take care of myself."

"Now, Levi, give me that money," added uncle Nathan, — and he looked as though he intended to renew the battle, — "and some of it shall go to pay for the mischief you've done here;" and again he glanced sadly at the broken crockery ware which Mrs. Fairfield was gathering up.

"I'll pay for it, if you'll let me alone," answered Levi, retreating towards the door.

"I'll let you alone when you give me that money! Do you think I'm going to let a boy like you fool away twenty-one dollars?"

"I'm going to fool it away in buying some clothes that I need."

"No, you ain't," replied the miser, testily. "I'll have that money, if I have to take it out of your hide."

"See here, uncle Nathan," continued Levi, in a conciliatory tone, — for such a quarrel was intensely disagreeable to him, — "I'm willing to do what's fair and right. I'll give you the money, if you'll agree to give me some decent clothes, and let me go to school."

"I won't agree to nothin' of the sort. The money belongs to me to take care on; and if you don't give it to me, I'll send a constable after you."

"Send him along," replied Levi, defiantly, as he left the house.

"I don't know what we're comin' to!" exclaimed Mrs. Fairfield. "That boy'll be the death on us."

"He shall give me that money," replied uncle Nathan, shaking his head.

"You must be a little kinder easy with him; then he'll give it to you. Why didn't you wait till he'd gone to bed, and then take it out of his pocket?"

"He shall give it to me. It's high time sunthin was done when a boy like him is goin about town with twenty-one dollars in his pocket."

"Wait till he goes to bed, and then you can git it."

"He'll spend it before that time. The boy has no more idee of the vally of money than he has of the man in the moon. He must be looked after. The next thing we shall know, he'll be drinkin rum, and gamblin; and then folks will say I didn't take good care on him."

"So they will," replied the sympathizing helpmate. "You must git that money by hook or by crook. It'll spile the boy, as sure as —— Goodness gracious! if there ain't Ruel!"

The last remark was called forth by the appearance of an elderly man, who had entered the back door without the preliminary of knocking. Ruel

Belcher was Mrs. Fairfield's brother. He was dressed in his Sunday clothes, and apparently he had come to pay his sister a visit. She and her husband shook hands with him, and wanted to know what the news was "over to Salem." Ruel told the news, and imparted the gratifying information that his wife and children were in good health, which uncle Nathan and his wife were glad to "hear on."

"Go'n to stop long with us?" asked Nathan, who had already begun to think whether or not he should be obliged to purchase a beefsteak from the under side of the round — a luxury he was compelled to have when company came.

"No, I'm going back to-night, if I can get through my business," replied Ruel.

"Law sake! you never stop none," said Mrs. Fairfield.

Mr. Fairfield was glad he did not — beef was high.

"I just run down to collect some money Dock Vincent owes me," added Ruel Belcher.

"How much does he owe you?" asked uncle Nathan, curiously.

"Two .hundred and fifty dollars. I was told, if I

5 *

came down now, I might get it; and I'm going to do it, if I have to jug him."

"Dock is a pretty hard man to git money out of," said Mr. Fairfield.

"Where's your boy?—Levi, I mean."

"He's just gone out."

Ruel wanted to see him about Dock Vincent, and it came out, to the visitor's great astonishment, that Levi was a very bad boy; that he had actually earned twenty-one dollars, and refused to give it to his honored guardian. To the surprise, not to say horror, of the "guardeen" and his wife, Ruel, after he had heard the whole story, rather sided with Levi. He wanted to see the boy, and volunteered to "talk" with him.

There was nothing in the house fit for a guest to eat, and dinner was delayed. While Ruel went to look for Levi, uncle Nathan, sorely exercised by the bitter necessity, started for the provision store in the village to procure a slice of beefsteak from the under side of the round.

As Levi walked away from the house, he felt that the two hundred and seventy-one dollars in his pocket was not safe upon his person. He anticipated the very action which Mrs. Fairfield had suggested; therefore he went down to the rocky cove where he kept his dory, and concealed it with great care in the crevice of a rock, upon which he heaped a pile of stones.

Before he had fully completed the work, Ruel Belcher joined him, shook hands with him, and treated him very kindly.

"I hear you have twenty-one dollars, Levi," said Ruel, laughing.

"I have, and I mean to keep it — at least till I can buy some clothes and things I want," replied Levi.

Ruel did not blame him; he gave him some good advice, and even volunteered to "talk" with the old man, and induce him to do better by his nephew.

"Now, I want to find Dock Vincent, Levi," said Ruel.

"He's going to Gloucester this afternoon in his schooner — there she lays," replied Levi, pointing to the vessel.

"He owes me some money, and I'm going to get it to-day."

"He can pay you, I guess; he made a hundred dollars this morning."

"I'm glad to hear that."

"How much does he owe you?" asked Levi.

"Two hundred and fifty dollars."

The young fisherman glanced at the heap of stones under which the price of The Starry Flag was concealed, and perhaps thought it a little odd that Dock owed Ruel just that sum.

CHAPTER V.

LEVI FAIRFIELD'S CHAMBER.

LEVI gave Ruel Belcher such information as he needed in regard to Dock's vessel, and the ability of its owner to pay a just debt of two hundred and fifty dollars.

"Now, Levi, we will go up and get some dinner, and then I will attend to Dock's case," said Ruel.

"I think I shall not go up to the house yet a while. Uncle Nathan will give me fits if I do."

"No, he won't: you must have your dinner."

"If I don't have it, this won't be the first time I've gone without my dinner."

"Do you mean to say that your uncle would not give you your dinner?"

"Well, I sit down to the table sometimes when there isn't enough on it for me, let alone three of us."

"I know he is mean."

"Mean! That word isn't big enough to say what you want to on that subject," replied Levi, with emphasis. "He would boil a wooden skewer to get the grease out of it. I suppose, if I should starve to death, he would have the money that is coming to me."

"Of course he don't mean anything of that sort."

"I don't know that he does, but I don't believe he would cry his eyes out if I should die to-night."

"Perhaps not, but he wouldn't do anything to help you off."

"I think he is doing it now. I don't like to say much about it, but I don't always get enough to eat. It is scrimp, scrimp, scrimp, from one year's end to the other. I've stood this thing about as long as I'm going to. I mean to have a little money about me, and when there's no meat on the bones at home, I'm going up to the eating-house, and have my dinner."

"Don't you make it out a little worse than it is, Levi?"

"No, sir! I haven't told you half."

"The folks always seem to live well enough when I've been here."

"Perhaps they do; but I'd like to have company all the year round," added Levi.

"I'll inquire into this business before I go, Levi, if you will help me find Dock Vincent after dinner."

"I'll be here when you come down."

"No, go up and have your dinner," persisted Ruel.

"I don't want to make any trouble. If uncle Nathan will only let me alone, I will look out for myself."

"He will."

Levi was persuaded to go to the house, and in due time was helped to a small portion of the "under side of the round;" and the young fisherman thought it was a great deal tougher where there was none, as his experience fully demonstrated. Ruel was in a hurry, and nothing was said about the affray in the kitchen; it was left till the more important business of the day had been disposed of.

After dinner Levi showed Ruel where to find his debtor, and he found him; but Dock declined to pay. A lawyer was obtained, a writ issued, and Dock's vessel was duly attached, just as he was on the point of starting for Gloucester, where he was going to load a freight for Boston. Dock was mad; he was in danger of losing a profitable job; and, about five in the afternoon, he paid the debt and sailed for his destined port. When Ruel had the money in his pocket, he found it was too late to return to Salem that night, and he was compelled to accept the hospitality of his brother-in-law.

Levi had no opportunity to visit Gloucester and buy The Starry Flag that day, but he determined to get up before daylight the next morning, and walk over, so as to have the advantage of the tide in going down the bay.

"Have you talked to that boy, Ruel?" said uncle Nathan, after supper.

"Yes, I said something to him," replied the brother-in-law, glancing at Levi.

"He needs seein to; he's got so we can't do nothin with him," added the guardian, sternly. "He finds fault with his victuals, wants to dress up like a dandy, and tips the table over."

"I didn't tip it over," said Levi, as calmly as he could.

"Don't tell me!"

"Well, I didn't, uncle Nathan," protested the young fisherman.

"Don't deny it again, sir. You know you did!"

"You pushed me on it."

"Do you hear that, Ruel?" added uncle Nathan, appealing to the visitor. "He contradicts me just as though I wan't nobody. He don't seem to know what a guardeen is for."

"I think I do," replied Levi, significantly.

"That boy's got twenty-one dollars in his pocket; and he won't give it to me."

"Let him have it then," laughed Ruel.

"Let him have it!" exclaimed Mr. Fairfield, with an exhibition of something like horror on his skinny face.

"Yes, let him have it. He is fifteen years' old, and ought to know enough not to fool it away."

"He don't."

"I only want it to buy some clothes," added Levi.

"He don't need no clothes. He's got a good suit up stairs."

"Why don't he wear it, then?" suggested Ruel.

"Them's his Sunday clothes."

"I want to put them on for every day," added Levi.

"To go a fishin and work in the dirt in!" ejaculated Mrs. Fairfield. Sakes alive! what are we comin to!"

"I want to wear them about town; I shall put on my old clothes to fish in," said Levi.

"You don't need no clothes. Them you got on is good enough," protested the miser.

"I don't think they are, Nathan," added Ruel. "They are nothing but rags and tatters. He went down town with me to-day, and I'm free to say I was ashamed of his looks."

"Well, he ought to put on his best clothes when we have company."

"I don't know as I want to say anything more about it now," said Ruel, glancing at Levi. "I see you don't agree very well, and I don't want to make things any worse."

"He's a bad boy; I don't know what he's comin to, if something ain't done," added Mr. Fairfield. "To think he should keep that money when I told him to give it to me — me, his guardeen."

"I guess I'll go to bed; I'm going to get up pretty early," continued Levi, who saw that Ruel had something to say which he did not wish to say before him.

"I don't know as you've got room enough for me to-night," suggested the visitor, who knew that there was no "spare room" in the house.

"Yes, we have, if you are willin to sleep with Levi. It's a wide bed," added Mrs. Fairfield.

"O, yes, I can sleep with Levi, if he is willing."

"You are welcome to sleep with me," replied Levi.

Uncle Nathan looked as though it did not make much difference whether he was willing or not, and Levi went to his room, leaving Ruel Belcher, whom he already regarded as his friend, to plead his cause before his uncle and aunt.

Ruel was faithful to the duty of the hour. He knew Nathan Fairfield well enough to believe that

Levi, in his complaints, had uttered no more than
the truth; and he was sorry to be compelled to
acknowledge that his sister had adopted the views
of her husband. He spoke very plainly of the boy's
affairs, and declared that he had a right to be sup-
ported in a manner corresponding to his property.

The guardian listened impatiently to the reproof.
He was angry that his brother-in-law, for whose use
and benefit he had actually expended twenty-five
cents in the purchase of a slice of the "under side
of the round," should presume to take part with the
boy, and condemn his guardian. It was impolite
and ungrateful.

"I'm saying what I do for your sake quite as much
as for the boy's," protested Ruel, when he found that
his advice was ungraciously received.

"You're takin sides with the boy, and encouragin
him to treat me as he does," replied Mr. Fairfield.

"Levi says he won't stand this any longer; and if I
know human nature, he won't," added Ruel. "There's
fight in him, and he can make a good deal of trouble
for you."

"Sho!" exclaimed the matron.

"He's made trouble enough already," added.her husband.

"He can go to the probate court, or get somebody to do it for him; and if he can prove half he says, the judge would remove you so quick it would make your head swim," added Ruel, decidedly.

"You don't say!" ejaculated Mrs. Fairfield.

"I ain't afeerd of nothin of that sort," said Nathan. "He's a bad boy. Why, he fit me like a tiger to-day."

"All this is none of my business; but I give it to you as my advice that you had better not meddle with him. If he earns any money, let him have it."

"Let him keep the twenty-one dollars?"

"Yes; and see what he does with it. If he uses it well, let him have what he earns."

"Ruel Belcher, you don't understand that boy!" said.Nathan, impressively. "I tell you he's a bad boy, and he's goin to ruin as fast as he can go."

"Let him alone, and then we shall see. If he spends his earnings foolishly, it will be time enough to stop him then."

"He'll fool away every cent of that money."

6*

"Wait and see. I think I'm about tired enough to go to bed now," added Ruel, rising from his chair. "I've got considerable money about me, you know; do you think it will be safe?"

"I s'pose it will be. There's nobody here to steal it, unless Levi does; and I'm afeerd he ain't none too good to do sich a thing."

"O, Levi is honest!" replied Ruel.

"I hope he is," added uncle Nathan.

Ruel Belcher took a lamp and went up to the little, low, dingy chamber, which had served before Levi's advent into the family as a "spare room," though, since it had been devoted to the use of the ward, most of the furniture had been removed, or exchanged for meaner articles from other parts of the house.

"Asleep, Levi?" asked the guest, as he entered the room.

"No, sir, not yet."

"Well, I've been talking over your affairs with your uncle, and I hope you will have less reason to complain," added Ruel — he hoped so, perhaps, but he hardly believed it would be so.

"I am much obliged to you, I'm sure," answered Levi. "I only want what is fair and right. I'm willing to work for my board, though uncle Nathan has an allowance of three dollars a week for my support."

"I know he does: be peaceable, Levi, if you can."

"I will; I don't want to have any trouble."

"I've got considerable money about me, Levi; do you think it will be safe?" continued Ruel, changing the subject.

"I don't know who could take it here."

"I guess it will be all right. I'll put it under my pillow."

Ruel deposited his wallet in the place indicated, and got into bed. He was tired, and in a short time both he and Levi were sound asleep. Half an hour later uncle Nathan entered the room in his stocking-feet, and after fumbling over the garments of both the sleepers for some time, he retired as noiselessly as he had entered.

What other events transpired in that chamber before the dawn of the day were known to no one in the house.

At four o'clock Levi got up, dressed himself in his best clothes, and left the room without waking Ruel Belcher.

When the guest rose, two hours later, his two hundred and fifty dollars was gone!

CHAPTER VI.

WHO STOLE THE WALLET?

IT was six o'clock when Ruel Belcher rose from
his bed, and wondered how he could have slept
so long; but he concluded that the fatigue and excitement of collecting a bad debt were the cause,
and as he was dressing he congratulated himself
upon his good fortune in obtaining his money; and
considering the character and antecedents of Dock,
he had abundant reasons for doing so. Ruel was a
hard-working carpenter, and by no means a rich
man. The two hundred and fifty dollars, therefore,
was a large sum of money to him; and as he had
had no expectation of collecting it, he was peculiarly
happy in its possession.

As he put on his clothes, he could not help thinking what a pleasure it would be to tell his wife that
he had the money in his pocket; and as the thought

passed through his mind, he went to the bed and
raised the pillow under which he had placed his
wallet.

It was not there.

Ruel was alarmed. He pulled out the pillows and
bolster, shook the bedclothes, turned the mattress,
and searched in every place he could think of for
the lost treasure. It was certainly gone. Ruel was
in despair. What a story this would be to tell his
wife! He felt cheap and mean to think he had
been "smart" enough to collect the money, and had
then lost it. He finished dressing himself, and then
made another thorough search for the wallet, but
with no better success than before.

He went down stairs, and announced his loss to
his sister. She was quite sure it must be somewhere
in the room, and she went up and searched for it.
Then Mr. Fairfield came in, and, being informed of
the loss, he went up and searched for it; but the
wallet was not to be found.

"I can't think what's become on't," said Mrs. Fairfield, greatly perplexed.

"Nor I either," replied Ruel. "I was dreaming

of that money last night, now I think of it. It seemed to me I got scared about it. I had an idea some one was coming into the room to take it away from me."

"Perhaps you wasn't asleep," suggested Mrs. Fairfield, glancing at her husband.

"O, I slept like a rock. I didn't know a thing from the time I went to sleep till six o'clock this morning," added Ruel.

"Perhaps you kinder half waked up when Nathan went into your room," continued the matron.

"Did he come into the room?"

"Yes, I went in about 'leven o'clock," added Mr. Fairfield.

"Well, I didn't hear you."

"Perhaps you sort o' waked, and, seein' Nathan, thought you dreamed it," explained Mrs. Fairfield.

"It may have been so, but I don't think it was. What did you come into the room for, Nathan?" asked Ruel.

"I hope you don't think I took your money!" exclaimed Mr. Fairfield.

"Of course I don't think anything of that sort."

Ruel did not believe his brother-in-law had robbed him, though he could not help thinking that such a thing was possible with a man who loved money as Nathan did.

"I'll tell you how it was, Ruel," continued Mr. Fairfield, not a little embarrassed by the circumstances which appeared to conspire against him. "As Levi's guardeen, I think twenty-one dollars is too much for him to have."

"So do I," interposed Mrs. Fairfield, willing to justify her husband. "It's a shame for him to behave as he does. He knows more'n his uncle now, and if sunthin ain't done, the boy'll go to ruin right off."

"I didn't mean Levi should fool away that money, no how; and I went up stairs for it, after he had gone to sleep. That's the long and short of the whole matter."

"That's the truth, you may depend upon't," added his sympathizing spouse.

"Did you get the money?" asked Ruel, curiously.

"No, I didn't."

"I suppose not."

"I sarched all his pockets, but I couldn't find nothin on't."

"Levi isn't a fool," added Ruel.

"What do you mean by that?" demanded Nathan.

"After you tried to take his money away from him by force, he wouldn't be likely to bring it into the house again. But that's neither here nor there: my money's gone, if Levi's isn't, and I'd like to know what has become of it."

"So should I," said Mr. Fairfield.

"I can't think what has become on't," added Mrs. Fairfield. "Nobody couldn't git into the house to steal it. The doors were all bolted this mornin just as I left 'em last night, and none of the winders has been teched. I can't see through it at all."

"Nor I nuther," said Mr. Fairfield. "Two hundred and fifty dollars is a sight of money to lose."

"Where's Levi?" asked Ruel. "Perhaps he will know something about it. Where is he?"

"I don't know. I hain't seen the boy sence I got up. I s'pose he's gone off after dog-fish," replied Mrs. Fairfield.

"I hain't seen him nuther," added her husband.

7

"I went down after sunthin to eat, and hain't been about house till just now."

Uncle Nathan had actually purchased another slice from the under side of the round, that morning, and after the ingratitude of his brother-in-law in siding with Levi, taking twenty-five cents from his pocket for such a purpose was like taking out the best tooth in his head.

Ruel was nervous and uneasy about his money. He hoped Levi might know something about it, and he went to the cove to see if he was there. Levi was not there; but the dingy dory was, which proved that he had not gone after dog-fish. At seven o'clock the young fisherman had not returned. When Mrs. Fairfield went up stairs to make the bed, she saw the old clothes of Levi hanging in the closet; and then she made the astounding discovery that he had dressed himself in his Sunday suit.

"What can it mean?" exclaimed she, after she had announced the significant fact to her husband and the guest.

"It means that he has gone off," replied Mr. Fairfield.

"Gone off!" repeated Ruel.

"Run away," added Nathan.

"Perhaps he is round town somewhere now."

"I guess not. What did he dress himself up for? Why didn't he come home to breakfast? If he dressed up for company, why don't he stay and see the company?" continued the guardian of Levi, piling up his interrogatory arguments, until the poor boy seemed to be crushed and condemned beneath the weight of them.

There was something like triumph apparent in the tones and the manner of Nathan Fairfield, as he heaped up the evidence against his nephew. Ruel could not think now, with all these indications of Levi's guilt, that he — his brother-in-law — had taken his money. Besides, he had labored hard on the preceding evening to show that Levi was a bad boy; Ruel would not believe it, and it was pleasant to have his statement proved to be correct, especially at the expense of the unbeliever.

"I didn't think Levi was a bad boy," said Ruel, musing. "He didn't seem like one to me, and I rather liked him."

"I cal'late you'll believe what I say another time," replied Nathan. "Levi's a bad boy; and he's been goin on from bad to wus, till no one can tell what'll become on him. I s'pose you know what's come of your money now."

"I hope Levi didn't take it," answered Ruel; and he really did hope so, even while it seemed to be impossible to doubt the fact.

"That boy must be taken care on. 'Tain't no use to let him run on any longer," added the guardian.

"What can we do?"

"We must find him first. I think we'd better have him taken up, and then we can tell what's best to be done," replied Nathan.

"Before we do that, we had better look round town, and see if we can find him."

"He ain't in town now, you may depend on't. He's gone off."

Ruel was not so positive, and an hour was spent in searching the vicinity for the fugitive. He was not to be found, and by nine o'clock a warrant for the arrest of Levi, on the charge of robbing his bed-fellow of two hundred and fifty dollars, was taken out, and placed in the hands of an officer, who immediately went to Gloucester in search of the alleged robber.

Nathan Fairfield groaned in spirit on that day, for Ruel Belcher appeared to be quartered upon him for several days; and what pounds of the under side of the round he would consume! What quantities of hot biscuit he would devour! What ounces of cheap tea he would pour down! What spoonfuls of brown sugar he would use! It was really appalling, and not even the satisfaction of proving that Levi was a rascal could compensate for such an inroad upon his domestic economy. Leaving him to groan in anguish over his visitor's terrific appetite, we will return to the unfortunate youth, over whom the clouds of wrath were gathering thick and black.

Levi got up at daylight, and dressed himself in his best clothes, for the visit to Gloucester. He hoped that the influence of Ruel Belcher would have some effect upon his lot; that his uncle would permit him to have and to enjoy his extra earnings in peace. He felt grateful to the guest for the interest he had manifested in him, and if he had

7 *

dared to do so, he would have told him all about
the money he had concealed in the rocks, and all
about his plan to buy The Starry Flag.

Levi dressed himself very carefully, so as not to
disturb the visitor. He did not like to go away and
leave him, for Ruel had seemed like a friend; but
The Starry Flag might be sold if there was any
delay. Besides, he hoped to return before the guest
departed, and thus secure his influence in reconciling
his guardian to the new boat. With a light step
he. descended the stairs, and left the house, passing
out through the cellar door, which fastened with a
wooden spring; for, when Ruel had so much money
about him, he did not think it was safe to leave the
back door unbolted.

The thought of the guest's money made him
inquire whether his own was safe. He had left it
out doors, because it would be more secure than
under the same roof with his guardian; but he had
some doubts. Dock Vincent might have watched
him when he concealed the wallet. His heart rose
up into his throat at the very thought; but he
hastened down to the cove. The *cache* he had

made had not been disturbed, and after removing the stones he had heaped upon it, he took the wallet from the crevice in the rock. It was all right, and his heart leaped with exultant joy.

With a light step he walked through the village, and took the road to Gloucester. As he trudged along, bright visions lighted up his vivid imagination, and he pictured to himself the pleasure he should derive from sailing The Starry Flag. If his uncle did not treat him well, or would not allow him to enjoy his own earnings, he could even live on board the boat; for there was a cuddy large enough for him to sleep in.

There would be an "awful tempest," when uncle Nathan found he had bought the boat; but Levi was prepared for the worst. He was determined not to be "ground down" any longer. If his guardian would not make a man of him, he would make a man of himself.

Thus dreaming of the future, and thus preparing his mind for the wrath of his guardian, he entered Gloucester, and soon found the wharf where The Starry Flag lay.

CHAPTER VII.

OFF EASTERN POINT.

IT was half past five in the morning when Levi
Fairfield reached the wharf in Gloucester, all un-
suspicious of the mischief which his unexplained
departure from home was to occasion. The Starry
Flag lay in the water near the shop of her benev-
olent builder, who had not yet come to his daily
work. As nothing could be done to forward the
business, Levi devoted himself to an examination of
the beautiful craft. Hauling in the painter, he went
on board, and carefully scrutinized every part of her.

The Starry Flag was twenty-one feet long, sloop
rigged, and had a cuddy forward, which contained
two berths. She was built in the most substantial
manner, and had already proved herself to be a stiff
and stanch sea-boat. She worked admirably in a
heavy sea, and it was even said that she could be

worked to windward under her jib alone. It is true she was not what would be called a "fancy yacht;" she had no mahogany panels, no elaborate brass work, no gilded figure-head. She was plain and neat, with little or no "gingerbread work" about her. It was her fine model, and her graceful sitting upon the water, that made her a beautiful craft.

Levi glowed with enthusiasm as he surveyed the boat — as he examined the construction and arrangement of everything about her. He crawled into the cuddy, which was just high enough to permit him to sit down on the berth, though, for the size of the craft, it was quite a roomy apartment, and large enough to accommodate himself and one other very comfortably. It was not furnished, and while the prospective owner of The Starry Flag was debating with himself whether he should spend his twenty-one dollars in the purchase of a couple of mattresses, or in procuring a suit of clothes, he heard a step upon the wharf.

"What are you doing in that boat?" demanded the owner.

"I was only looking at her," replied Levi.

"We don't allow folks on board of her, unless they want to buy her."

"That's just my case," added Levi, as he stepped upon the wharf.

"I reckon you don't exactly know what you are talking about," said Mr. Hatch, the builder, as he measured the boy from head to foot with his eye.

"I reckon I do, Mr. Hatch. I came over from Rockport on purpose to buy her, if you will let me have her for what's about right."

"You?"

"I'm your man, Mr. Hatch. I know you, if you don't know me. If you want to sell this boat for a fair price, I want to buy her."

"I rather think she will cost too much for you. She's a nice boat."

"I know she is; and that's the reason I want to buy her. I shouldn't want her if she wasn't a nice boat. What do you ask for her?"

"Two hundred and fifty; and she's as cheap as dirt at that."

"Won't you take two hundred for her?"

"I won't take a cent less than I said, for you see

the money 's for the new church over in your town."

Levi offered two hundred and twenty-five; but Mr. Hatch thought it would be cheating " the treasury of the Lord" to take anything less than the price, and he was inflexible. '

" I'll take her, sir," said Levi, when he had exercised all his Yankee shrewdness in trying to make a good bargain.

" It seems to me you are pretty young to buy a boat like this," said the builder, good-naturedly.

" Perhaps I am; but I've got the money, and I suppose that is all you want," answered Levi.

" Well, no; that isn't all I want. Boys like you don't very often have two hundred and fifty dollars to spend for a boat, and I want to know that it's all right before I let her go. What's your name?"

" Levi Fairfield."

" You are not Captain Fairfield's boy — are you?"

" Yes, sir; I live at Rockport with my uncle Nathan."

" Yes, I know you do; and I don't know as that helps the matter much," added Mr. Hatch, with a significant chuckle. "Nathan Fairfield's your guardian and I suppose it would be just about as easy to jump over the moon as it would be for him to give you money enough to buy this boat."

"He didn't give it to me."

"I supposed not," laughed the boat-builder. "Where did you get the money?"

Levi explained where he got it.

"I guess it's all right, Levi," added Mr. Hatch. "Mr. Ames, the minister, was over here yesterday afternoon, and told me a boy saved a girl from drowning; but I had no idea you were the young fellow."

"Mr. Watson let me have the money on purpose to buy this boat, and you may depend upon it, the matter is all straight."

"Then the boat is yours. Come into the shop with me, and I will make out a bill of sale of her."

The bill was made out, and Levi paid over the two hundred and fifty dollars, with the feeling that The Starry Flag was dog-cheap at that price. Mr. Hatch was much pleased with the purchaser, and when the trade was completed, he invited him to take breakfast with him. Levi accepted the invitation, and finding a much better table than that to which he was accustomed at the house of his guardian, he did ample justice to the generous fare of his host.

Though the stores were now open in the town, Levi, anxious to reach Rockport before the departure of Ruel Belcher, concluded to defer the purchase of his clothes till another day. Full of joy and exultation, he embarked in the boat, which he could now call his own, cast off the painter, pushed off, and with the best wishes of Mr. Hatch, started on his voyage round the cape. The tide was going out, but there was hardly a breath of wind to swell the sails he spread. Unless he found a breeze outside of the harbor, he could hardly expect to reach Rockport before afternoon; but he hoped for the best. With a fresh wind the boat would make the distance in a couple of hours.

When two hours had elapsed, The Starry Flag had hardly reached Norman Woe Reef, which lies at the entrance of Gloucester Harbor. As there was now no possibility of getting home before the depart-

8

ure of Ruel, the young fisherman gave up the hope
of doing so, and began to consider how he should
conduct his defence before his guardian. Ahead of
him lay a small schooner, which he recognized as the
Griffin, Dock Vincent's vessel. She had probably
been becalmed during the night, and could not get
up the bay against the tide.

Levi did not care to meet Dock just then, especially after the assistance he had rendered Ruel in
collecting his debt. He wanted to sheer off, and
avoid him; but there was not a particle of wind, and
the boat was drifting helplessly with the tide, which
bore him directly alongside of the Griffin.

"Hallo, Levi! What are you doing here?" demanded Dock, from the deck of his vessel.

"Going home."

"Is that The Starry Flag?"

"Yes."

"What are you doing with her?"

"I've bought her, and she's mine now," replied
Levi, with a feeling of pride and satisfaction.

"Have you, though?"

"Just bought her, and paid for her."

"Come aboard — will you? I want to talk with you," added Dock.

"I can't stop now; I want to get home."

"You might as well stop where you are till a breeze of wind comes. When you get outside of Eastern Pint, the tide will set you back."

Levi knew this to be true, and he hauled up alongside the Griffin. Dock did not manifest any resentment towards him on account of the debt, and Levi wished to inform him what Mr. Watson had done, in order to free the rich merchant from the imputation of meanness which Dock cast upon him.

"So you've bought The Starry Flag — have you?" continued Dock, when Levi stepped upon the deck of the Griffin.

"I have — gave two hundred and fifty dollars for her. I promised to tell you to-day what Mr. Watson did for me."

"He gave you two hundred and fifty dollars — did he?"

"He offered to give it to me, but I didn't like to take it for picking up a drowning girl; so I borrowed it of him."

"Borrowed it! I say, Levi, you are a fool!"
sneered Dock. "That man ought to have given
you a thousand dollars at the very least; and you
were a fool to let him off for anything less than
that."

"If I am satisfied with what he has done, I don't
think anybody else has a right to complain," replied
Levi, with considerable spirit.

For an hour, Dock labored to convince the young
fisherman that he had been grievously wronged and
cheated by the wealthy merchant from Boston; but
Levi, happy in the possession of The Starry Flag,
refused to be convinced. Mr. Watson had done "the
handsome thing," in his opinion, and so far from feeling any dissatisfaction, he was deeply grateful to
him.

"If you don't know your rights, Levi, I'm not
going to teach you," continued Dock. "According
to your own story, Watson didn't give you anything.
He paid you ten dollars for the fish you lost, and
lent you two hundred and fifty dollars."

"I don't suppose he expects me to pay him back
what I borrowed, but I mean to do so," added Levi.

"Then Watson didn't give you anything?"

"No, but —"

"That's all I want to know. Now, Levi, I've got a bone to pick with you."

"What's that?"

"You served me a mean trick yesterday."

"I didn't serve you any mean trick," protested Levi.

"Yes, you did; you helped Belcher get that money out of me."

"You owed it to him — didn't you?"

"That's none of your business; I don't like to pay money till I get ready. I know just where I can trip you up, Levi, and I'm going to do it. I used to think you was a friend of mine, and would be willing to do me a good turn if you got a chance."

"Without claiming to be your friend, I'm willing to do you a good turn now," replied Levi.

"You are not; if you had told me Belcher was looking for me, I could have kept my vessel out of his way. You didn't do it; you helped Belcher, instead of me. I don't find no fault, Levi; you have chosen for yourself. If you don't want any-

8 *

thing of me, I don't want anything of you. I'm your enemy now."

"If you are, I can't help it."

"You'll get tripped up."

"If I am, I will pick myself up," said Levi, as lightly as he could; but he did not like to have such a man as Dock for an enemy.

"If you have a mind to join me in a little plan of mine that won't hurt nobody, I will —"

"I won't join you in any plan," interposed Levi, who, being honest, felt that he could afford to be independent.

"Just as you like, Levi; but look out for breakers!" said Dock, with a threatening shake of his head.

"There's a breeze coming, and I guess I'll be off," added Levi, as he jumped into his boat.

"Just remember what I've said to you; and when you want to see me, I'm round," said Dock.

The Starry Flag caught the first breath of the coming wind, and went off towards Eastern Point. Levi was annoyed by the threats of Dock, but he was resolved to be honest and true, come what might come. The boat worked well, and as she was rounding the Point, Levi was rather pleased to see a schooner boat making towards him, for it gave him the promise of a race.

That schooner boat contained the constable, with a warrant in his pocket for the arrest of Levi.

•

CHAPTER VIII.

THE TEMPEST AND THE WRECK.

LEVI FAIRFIELD had no suspicion of the tempest that was brewing over him at home, and of which the constable in the schooner boat was the forerunner; but he was weatherwise enough to see that a literal storm was gathering in the west, which might try the nerves of The Starry Flag, if it did not those of her bold-hearted skipper. The wind was now blowing a gentle breeze from the eastward, but vast volumes of dense black clouds were piling up in the opposite quarter. They were squally-looking clouds, and even a less experienced salt than the young fisherman might have known that there was wind in them.

There was no present danger, and Levi, determined to "keep his weather-eye open tight," watched with deep interest the movement of the schooner boat, which, by getting the breeze sooner than the Flag, had approached within a quarter of a mile. She was evidently following him, and he could conceive of no other purpose on the part of her skipper than that of "trying a race" with him.

Levi had a great deal of confidence in the sailing qualities of his boat; and after holding on his course to the northward for a time, he had the intense satisfaction of finding that the other boat did not gain upon him. But the race was not so exciting, at that distance, as it would be with the boats abreast of each other; and he put his helm down, throwing the Flag up into the wind for the purpose of waiting for his rival to come up.

The schooner boat bore down upon him, and in a few moments was within hailing distance, the boatman prudently keeping her well to windward, for he seemed to comprehend the fact that the Flag was the faster craft of the two. When she was fairly abreast of him, Levi filled away again, and began to be quite excited as the race opened.

"Levi!" shouted the constable in the schooner boat, when he saw that the chase was off again.

"Schooner ahoy!" shouted Levi, in reply.

"Levi!" repeated the officer.

"Hallo!" replied Levi, now recognizing Mr. Gayles, the constable, but without the remotest idea that the officer was after him in his official capacity.

"I want to see you," added Mr. Gayles.

"Want to race — don't you?"

"I'm after you."

"All right," answered Levi, who interpreted this remark to mean that he wished to catch him, nautically speaking. "Come along! I'm all ready for you."

The Flag gathered headway, and began to run away from the schooner boat at a rate which probably astonished the skipper of the latter as much as it delighted the skipper of the former.

"Hold on, Levi!" cried the constable.

"Can't stop," replied the young fisherman, so exhilarated by the race that he could think of nothing else.

If he had been guilty of any crime, he might have thought that the constable was after him. He knew Mr. Gayles very well; indeed, he was the man who bought the dog-fish livers of him, and he was anxious to prove to him that The Starry Flag was "the fastest boat out." He certainly established the fact that she could outsail the schooner boat, for in half an hour she was a quarter of a mile ahead of her rival, and the parties were no longer within speaking distance of each other. While they were in these relative positions, the wind suddenly died out, and the sails of both flapped loosely from the gaffs.

The black and angry clouds were travelling rapidly up to the zenith. The morning had been intensely warm, and the air was "close" and oppressive. It was one of those days which seem to invite a tumult in the elements; one of those days which wind up with a squall, a hurricane, or an earthquake. Both the schooner and the sloop now lay helpless upon the water, rising and falling on the long rollers which throbbed and throbbed with glassy surfaces till they were dashed to pieces on the rocky coast.

The calm was the prelude of a storm. The lightnings glared upon the darkened waters, and the heavy thunders roared and rattled. The sun was shut in by the inky clouds, and it looked like coming night upon the ocean. All was still and quiet in the boats, except the swaying of the sails, as the little craft rolled on the glassy billows.

Levi ceased to regard the schooner boat as a rival, and now gazed earnestly to the westward, from which the shower was coming up. He improved these idle moments in lowering and stowing his jib, for he was almost sure of a heavy squall. Glancing at the other boat, he saw that she had taken in her jib and mainsail, and that the two men in her were rowing towards him. He then examined his mainsail halyards to make sure they were not foul, so that he could pull down the sail in an instant, if necessary.

While he was thus engaged, a dull, heavy roar from shoreward attracted his attention. It increased in volume, and seemed to travel like the lightning. Levi needed no second warning, but, casting off the halyards, hauled down the sail as rapidly as though his life depended upon the celerity of his movements; and, indeed, it did.

The squall came down upon the boats with appalling speed and violence, and Levi had only time to adjust a couple of the "stops" on his mainsail before it struck the Flag, and she careened under the blast till the young fisherman began to fear that she would go over, even with no sail upon her. It was by far the heaviest squall he had ever seen, amounting almost to a tornado. Levi saw that the heeling over of the boat was caused by a portion of the sail taking the wind. It was impossible to stand up, so savage was the tempest; but he succeeded in loosening the topping lift, and bringing the boom down so that he could secure the truant canvas.

The squall continued for several minutes,—they seemed like hours to the young boatman,—and terrific were the roaring and howling of the blast, the crash of the thunder, and the blinding glare of the lightning. It was awful, even to one accustomed to the sea when the elements rage in their wildest fury. It was one of those moments when nothing human seems to be abiding, and man leans upon the arm of God, who manifests His power and loftiest majesty in the sublimity of the fierce temp'

The squall was over in two or three whe mainsail the Storm King appeared not to be a part of the

9

842121 A

the tumult he had created; and though the terrific blast subsided, the wind still blew a gale from the westward, as though there were still empty chambers to be filled by the cooling currents. As the tempest of winds subsided, the rain began to pour down in torrents, and Levi's Sunday suit was soon drenched. He had closed up his cuddy to keep it dry; but he dared not take shelter within, lest the boat should come to harm for the want of a lookout.

"Help! help!"

The cry came to him through the thick mists formed by the rain near the surface of the water. He was thinking whether the schooner boat had weathered the squall, when these appalling sounds came to him above the howling of the gale. By this time the sea had been lashed into fury, and the waves were covered with white caps and flying spray.

"Help! help!" came the wail again through the ~~mist~~ and the rain.

ments; ~~ght~~ have been repeated twenty times, for The squ. ment before, the voice, if it had been ing speed an tor, could not have been heard above the roar of the storm. The Flag was now leaping and pitching in the angry sea, occasionally dipping in the water over her wash-board, while the spray dashed furiously upon her half deck.

A cry of distress touches the sailor's heart, and Levi had enough of the spirit of the true seaman to be deeply moved by the summons; but the tempest was still fearful, and it was little better than madness for him to hoist his mainsail.

"Help! help!" again came the tones of the sufferers through the storm; and this time it sounded like a voice from a sepulchre.

Levi could not resist the appeal, for he felt that it would be better to die in a noble and manly effort to save his fellow-beings in distress, than to lie idly by, counting up the perils of the attempt. Taking off the stops, he hastily put two reefs in his mainsail, though the work was not accomplished until the hailing cry had been several times repeated. With much doubt and anxiety he hoisted the sail.

The wind came in furious blasts, and the mainsail beat and threshed as though it were part of the storm. The halyards, carefully secured, and the ends coiled down so that they would not foul if it were again necessary suddenly to reduce sail, he dodged the swaying boom, and reached the helm. Hauling in the main sheet, the wind filled the sail, heeling the boat over till the water rushed in over the lee side. The intrepid young skipper "eased her off" a little, and she righted; and then she darted off, leaping over the wild waves as if in utter contempt of their impotent fury.

Levi now had the Flag under perfect control, and she flew towards the wreck from which proceeded the drowning cry of the two men. When the blast came too fresh, he eased off the sheet, giving the sail no more wind than it could safely carry. The boat behaved admirably, lifting herself on the billows, instead of plunging her nose down into them.

Levi strained his eyes to catch a glimpse, through the dense mists, of the men who needed his assistance; but he was quite near when he obtained his first view of them. The schooner boat had been upset, with her foresail still set. She was full of water, though she had partially righted; and not

AFTER THE SQUALL. Page 101.

being heavily ballasted, she did not go down. The foresail was flapping madly in the gale, and the two men were clinging to the wreck for their lives.

Levi rounded to under the stern of the disabled boat, and her skipper, seizing the bowsprit, leaped on board the Flag.

"Save me! save me!" cried the constable, in mortal terror, as he saw the Flag fall off, and drift out of his reach.

"I'll save you, Mr. Gayles. Hold on tight for a moment longer!" shouted Levi; and, hauling in his main sheet, he brought the Flag up again until the bowsprit was within the officer's reach.

"God bless you, Levi Fairfield!" exclaimed Mr. Gayles, as he crawled in over the bow, and made his way to the standing-room. "You have saved my life."

"I always pick up anything I find adrift," replied Levi, coolly.

9 *

CHAPTER IX.

AFTER THE SQUALL.

"THAT was a pretty tough one — wasn't it?" said the skipper of the schooner boat, referring to the squall.

"It was the hardest blow I was ever out in," replied Levi. "I don't know that I should want to try that over again."

"I shouldn't, either; it knocked my boat over quicker 'n a flash of lightning; I was rowing, and didn't mind much about it till it struck us. But it's beginning to moderate."

"It will be good weather pretty soon now; I think I can carry my sail with two reefs, and I shall stand on."

"I suppose you are bound to Rockport," continued the skipper, glancing at the constable.

"That's where I'm going; I suppose you are going there too," added Levi.

"Well, no; I don't know as I need to go there now. I want to save my boat, if you ain't in no hurry. I can't afford to lose her."

"I'll help you, if you like."

"Thank you. Mr. Gayles was after you —"

"Never mind that now," interposed the constable, who, drenched to the skin, and chilled through, sat on the weather side of the boat, shivering like a man with the ague.

"After me!" exclaimed Levi, with some astonishment.

"I wanted to see you," explained Mr. Gayles; "but it's no matter now."

Levi did not understand what the constable could wish to see him for; but the management of the boat required all his attention, and he could not press the question. He kept the Flag "off and on" for a short time, till the wind had subsided enough to allow the skipper to board his water-logged craft. The black clouds blew over almost as rapidly as they had come up, and though the sea was still angry, it was not violent.

The Flag was run up to the wreck; Levi and the

skipper jumped aboard, while Mr. Gayles was instructed to stand by with the boat-hook and keep
the boats from jamming each other in the sea. The
work of baling out the schooner boat commenced
with a bucket and a two-quart dipper belonging to
the Flag. It was a two hours' job, but the exercise
was very agreeable in the chilled state of the work-
men. As the operation proceeded, the schooner rose
in the water, and the skipper was the most grateful
of men when he realized that both his boat and his
life were preserved.

"Levi, if you want to get away from him, I'll
manage it for you," said the skipper, in a low tone,
when the water in the boat had fallen below the
thwarts.

"Get away from him! What do you mean?"
asked Levi, so astonished that he suspended his
work.

"Why, don't you know?"

"I'm sure I don't."

"They say you stole the money to buy your
boat."

"Stole it!" gasped Levi; "I'm sure I didn't."

"I don't know anything about it, but if you want to get rid of the constable, I'll help you do it. Hush! don't say a word, or he'll hear us."

"I didn't steal the money, and I don't want to get away from him. Then you were after me? I thought you only wanted to race."

"Well, I thought I could beat The Starry Flag."

"I stole the money!" repeated Levi, who under this startling accusation had lost his interest in racing.

"I hope it ain't true, Levi," added the sympathizing skipper.

"It is not."

"I'll get Gayles into this boat as soon as we have baled her out, and then you may go where you like."

"I shall face the music; I didn't steal the money, and I'm not afraid of any of them."

"That's right! I like your spunk."

"I'll take Mr. Gayles round to Rockport in my boat. I should like to see the man that says I stole the money."

"I don't know nothing about it, only what the constable says. He's got a warrant for you."

"Has he? I don't understand it."

Levi was so excited and indignant that he could not work any longer. The wind had subsided to a gentle breeze, the dark clouds had rolled away, and the sun was struggling out from the black mantle which had concealed it. The skipper volunteered to complete the work of baling out the boat himself, and to release the Flag from further attendance, so that she could proceed on her way round the cape.

"Who says I stole that money, Mr. Gayles?" demanded Levi, as he returned to the Flag.

"You mustn't blame me, Levi, for I hadn't anything to do with it. I'm very thankful to you for saving me, and I don't like — "

"But who says I stole the money?" repeated Levi, indignantly.

"Your uncle and Ruel Belcher both say so."

"Well, I didn't."

"I don't believe you did, Levi."

"I know I didn't."

"I'll tell you all about it as we go along. Do you think it is safe to go round in this boat?" asked the constable, as he glanced at the retreating clouds, from which the thunder still boomed in the distance.

"Safe enough," replied Levi, commencing mechanically to shake out the reefs in his mainsail.

The Flag had taken in considerable water during the squall and the blow that followed it, which Levi baled out, and then with his sponge wiped off the seats in the standing-room. The sun soon came out clear, and dried the boat so that she was clean and comfortable. Under all sail, the Flag stood on her course round the cape.

"I don't care what any one says; I didn't steal that money," said Levi, when he had put the boat in order, and seated himself at the weather side of the tiller.

"I don't know anything about it myself, Levi," replied Mr. Gayles, who was exceedingly embarrassed by the awkwardness of his position, for it was anything but pleasant for him to arrest the young man who had just saved his life. "The warrant was given to me with orders to arrest you. I am almost tempted to let you go now."

"I don't want you to let me go. I haven't done

anything; and I should like to see the man who
says I stole the money."

"I hope it will be all right when you explain
matters."

"Are you going to put me in jail?" asked Levi,
with a shudder.

"You needn't be alarmed, Levi; I'll see that you
are well treated. I'm responsible for your appearance
before the justice, and I think you and I can arrange
matters."

"Uncle Nathan and Ruel Belcher say I stole the
money," added Levi, trying to think what possible
foundation there was for such a charge.

"That's what they say."

"Whose money was it that was stolen?"

"Ruel Belcher's."

"He had two hundred and fifty dollars, and put it
under his pillow when he went to bed."

"And this morning it was gone," added Mr.
Gayles.

"Was it stolen?" asked Levi, to whom this intelligence was all new.

"The money was gone, and so were you. It was

found that you had dressed up in your Sunday clothes, and gone off without saying a word to anybody."

"That's true; but I didn't take Ruel's money — no, I wouldn't do that. If anybody took it, it was — Well, I won't say that, for I don't know anything about it."

He was going to mention his uncle's name.

"When it was found that you didn't come home to breakfast, they were sure you had the money. Your uncle stuck to it that you were bad enough to do such a thing," added Mr. Gayles.

"Perhaps he thinks so; he and I don't agree very well."

"No one is much surprised at that," said the constable, with a chilly smile.

"But I wonder what did become of Ruel's money," mused Levi.

"I felt pretty sure you had it, Levi, when I got over to Gloucester. I might as well tell you the worst. You had just bought this boat for exactly the sum Ruel had lost, as Mr. Hatch told me."

"Didn't he tell you where I got the money?"

"He told me you said Mr. Watson gave it to you for saving his daughter; but when I saw Dock Vincent on board his vessel, he said Mr. Watson didn't give you anything; you acknowledged that he didn't."

Levi then told Mr. Gayles the simple truth in regard to the whole transaction.

"Uncle Nathan tried to get my money away from me yesterday, but I didn't let him know that I had the two hundred and fifty dollars," he continued. "I knew he wouldn't let me buy the boat if I did."

"Where is Mr. Watson now?" asked the constable.

"He went off to Rye Beach yesterday, just as soon as they came out of the water."

"We want him as a witness: he can make the daylight shine through this matter in the twinkling of an eye," added the officer, now fully convinced that his bold deliverer was innocent of the foul charge.

We must do Mr. Gayles the justice to say that this conclusion was highly satisfactory to him.

Levi, confident that his innocence would be proved,

was very cheerful, and even laughed as he thought of the confusion which awaited his uncle.

The wind was not fresh enough for a quick passage, and it was the middle of the afternoon when The Starry Flag reached the head of the little cove, where the dingy dory was hauled up on the rocks. The landing-place was near the house of uncle Nathan; and before Levi could secure the Flag at her moorings, he was seen from the windows. The host and the guest hastened down to the cove.

"You've got him!" said Nathan Fairfield, with a gleam of satisfaction on his skinny face, as he glanced from the officer to his nephew.

"I don't know whether I've got him, or he's got me," replied Mr. Gayles, facetiously.

"Why don't you hold on to him, and put the irons onto him?" added the humane guardian.

"I shall put no irons on that boy, you may depend upon it."

"He's a bad boy, and he'll get away from you, as sure as you're alive," protested Mr. Fairfield. "Whose boat is that?"

"It belongs to Levi," replied Mr. Gayles. "He went over, to Gloucester this morning to buy her."

"With the money he stole!" exclaimed the guardian.

"I don't think he stole any money."

"Don't you?" sneered Mr. Fairfield. "And you say he bought that boat. What did he give for it?"

"I gave two hundred and fifty dollars for the boat; and I didn't steal the money to do it with, either," interposed Levi.

"Do you hear that, Ruel? Now you can see what that boy is!" ejaculated the guardian.

"Where did you get the money to pay for the boat?" asked Ruel.

Levi told the whole story about the two hundred and fifty dollars given him, or rather loaned, for the purchase of the boat.

"I don't believe a word on't!" exclaimed uncle Nathan. "Tell me! I know better. That boy stole the money from under your pillow, Ruel!"

"I hope he tells the truth," replied Ruel.

"I know he don't," protested Mr. Fairfield. "Mr. Gayles, why don't you take him up?"

"Come, Levi, we will walk up town, if you are ready," said the constable in a gentle and respectful tone.

"I'm ready," replied Levi; and he walked off with Mr. Gayles, to the great indignation of his uncle, who seemed to think he ought to be put in irons and dragged up to the bar of justice.

10 *

CHAPTER X.

DOCK VINCENT'S LITTLE PLAN.

WHAT are you going to do with me, Mr.
Gayles?" asked Levi, as he walked up the
road with the constable.

"If you hadn't saved my life to-day, I should put
you in the lock-up."

"I don't know that I saved your life. You would
have done well enough as long as you held on to
the boat. But what I did needn't make any difference," added Levi. "You can put me in jail, if you
like."

"But I don't like."

"I'm not afraid of a jail. I haven't done anything."

"I shall not put you in jail, Levi. I must take
you before a justice to-morrow, when you will be
examined."

"Well, what then?" asked Levi, curiously.

"If there is evidence enough to hold you, the justice will commit you for trial?"

"What then?"

"You will be tried before the court next week."

"What do you mean by commit me?"

"Commit you to jail to await your trial; but you can give bail."

"Perhaps I can," replied Levi, musing; "but I think my uncle would let me lie in jail a year before he would risk any money on me."

"I will see about your bail, Levi; but I hope there will be no need of any. If, at your examination before the justice to-morrow, you can prove to his satisfaction that you came honestly by the money you paid for the boat, you will be discharged."

"Perhaps I can't prove it. Mr. Watson went away yesterday morning."

"Do you know where he went?"

"To Rye Beach."

"That matter must be attended to at once," said Mr. Gayles, as they reached his house. "Come in, Levi."

"Is this the lock-up?" asked Levi, with a sickly smile.

"This is all the lock-up I shall take you to; I am responsible for your safe keeping."

"I won't run away, Mr. Gayles," protested the prisoner. "I'm going to stand up and face the music."

"I'm satisfied, Levi. We will make you as comfortable as we can here," added the constable, as they entered the house.

Mr. Gayles told his wife, as briefly as he could, what had happened since he left home in the morning; and the young fisherman was as welcome beneath that humble roof as though he had been the President, or the richest man in Rockport. He was treated like an honored guest, and not like a criminal. While Mrs. Gayles was cooking some ham and eggs for the dinner of the wanderers from the sea, the officer drew from Levi all the latter knew in regard to Mr. Watson. It was absolutely necessary that the attendance of the rich Boston merchant should be procured for the examination on the following day, for he was the only person by whom it could be proved where **Levi** obtained the money to purchase the boat.

"I have some money, Mr. Gayles — twenty-one dollars. I'll hand it over to you, and I want you to do everything that needs to be done for me," continued Levi, as he gave him his wallet.

"Do you want counsel?"

"Counsel?"

"A lawyer, to do the talking for you?"

"Just as you think best."

"I will see about that to-morrow. A good lawyer would be a great help to you; but if we can get Mr. Watson here, I don't think we shall need one."

After dinner, Mr. Gayles left the house, to send a special messenger to Rye for Mr. Watson. When he had gone, Ruel Belcher called to see the prisoner.

"Well, Levi, I'm sorry for this business," said Ruel.

"It will come out all right; you may be sure of that. I'm only sorry you think I stole your money," replied Levi.

"I didn't want to think so."

"I suppose uncle Nathan tried hard to make you believe it."

• "While I hope you didn't do it, Levi, I must say I think it looks bad for you."

"Maybe it does."

"You got up this morning, and went off without saying a word to anybody. You put on your best clothes; and when I got up, my money was gone. Now, it seems you have bought a boat for two hundred and fifty dollars — just the sum I lost."

"But it wasn't your money," added Levi, warmly. "Don't I say it was given to me by Mr. Watson — or rather lent to me — on purpose to buy that boat?"

"We don't know anything about Mr. Watson. Just when we want to see him, we find he has gone away."

"He has gone away, but he will be here again to-morrow, I hope."

"I don't like to be hard upon you, Levi, for I always rather liked you, and you have had a hard row to hoe with your uncle; but it looks to me just as though you made up this story to show where you got the money."

"I did get the money of Mr. Watson."

"But you told your uncle he gave you but ten dollars for the dog-fish you lost."

"That's all he *gave* me; he lent me the two hundred and fifty dollars."

"That's a pretty story! Do you mean to tell me a rich merchant, like Mr. Watson, would lend a boy, like you, two hundred and fifty dollars?" continued Ruel Belcher, sternly.

"I mean to say that is just what he did do," replied Levi, decidedly.

"Did you give him your note?" sneered Ruel.

"No, I didn't; he was in a hurry to go, and I had no time."

"Why didn't you tell of it last night?"

"I knew better than that. Uncle Nathan would have taken it away from me."

"He will do that now."

"Mr. Watson let me have the money to buy that boat."

"Who sold you the boat?"

"Mr. Hatch — and a nice man he is too."

"So they say; and I suppose he will give back the money you paid him for the boat."

"Give it back!" exclaimed Levi, almost paralyzed at the thought of losing The Starry Flag. "I don't want him to do that!"

"It don't make any difference whether you do or not. Your uncle started right off for Gloucester to get the money back as soon as you were taken up."

"Did he?" said Levi, bitterly.

"You can set your mind at rest about the boat, Levi; for your uncle, as your guardian, won't let you buy her."

"I have bought her, and she is mine."

"It's no use for you to talk in that way, Levi. I don't think there's any sense or reason in a boy like you owning a boat that costs so much money."

"I think I'm able to keep as good a boat as that."

"That may be: when you are of age, you can do what you like with your money; but you won't have that boat," replied Ruel. "Levi, this matter don't look right. The best thing you can do is to make a clean breast of it."

"I've told the truth. I haven't got your money, and I haven't had it."

"Where is it, then?"

"I don't know."

"Do you think your uncle took it?"

"I don't know anything about it."

Ruel could make nothing of the prisoner, and he went away, rather confirmed than otherwise in his belief that Levi had stolen the money.

In the evening, while Mr. Gayles was out, Dock Vincent, who was loading his vessel at Gloucester, and had come home to spend the night, paid the prisoner a visit. He was very anxious to see Levi alone, and they met in the constable's little parlor. The young fisherman could not imagine what Dock wanted of him; and he could not help calling to mind the threats the reckless skipper had used on board the Griffin that morning. Dock had declared that he was Levi's enemy; and to the young man it did not seem as though they could have any business together.

"Well, Levi, you have got into a bad scrape," said Dock.

"Perhaps I have."

"You will be lucky if you get off with six months in the House of Correction. It looks bad for you."

11

"It will look all right when Mr. Watson comes," replied Levi, cheerfully.

"Is he coming back?" asked Dock, apparently a little startled by the intelligence.

"We expect him."

"Perhaps he will come, Levi; but in my opinion he won't."

"What makes you think he won't?" asked Levi, anxiously.

"Why should he? What do you suppose he cares for you? He's a mean man."

"I don't think so."

"Well, no matter about that, Levi. I'm a witness in this case; and I think it depends more upon what I say than it does upon what anybody else says. I can get you out of this scrape quicker than you can say Jack Roberson."

"How?"

"Never mind that now," replied Dock, with a knowing nod of the head. "And a word from me will send you to the House of Correction for six months."

"I only want you to tell the truth," added Levi, again recalling the threat of Dock.

"That's what I expect to do, but it will spoil your case. I suppose you remember what you said to me off Eastern Point, this morning."

"What was it?"

"That Mr. Watson didn't give you anything for saving his daughter. That's right from your own mouth, Levi, and it's the truth, too."

Levi had said so to Dock and to his uncle; and, if Mr. Watson did not come to the examination, their evidence would certainly condemn him.

"But I told you Mr. Watson lent me the money," said Levi.

"Lent it to you!" laughed Dock. "I say, Levi, I wouldn't say a word about his lending the money to you. No one will believe it if you do."

Levi was really afraid no one would believe it, and he could not help being deeply depressed by the situation, for his own words were to be brought up to condemn him.

"Levi, you did me an ill turn yesterday, and I shall have a chance to get even with you to-morrow," continued Dock, satisfied with the effect he had already produced.

"Then you mean to give evidence against me," replied Levi, gloomily.

"That will depend upon circumstances. I suppose you didn't know I saw Mr. Watson give you the two hundred and fifty dollars?"

"Did you?"

"Nobody knows anything about it if I did; but you remember I joined you at the cove, just after Mr. Watson and his daughter went up to the house. You didn't see me, but perhaps I was within earshot of you when you were talking with him, and perhaps I heard all you said about borrowing the money."

"Did you hear it, Captain Dock?" demanded Levi, eagerly.

"I didn't say I did, and I didn't say I didn't; but you know I wasn't a mile off· while you were talking together."

"All I want is the truth."

"It is true that you told me Watson gave you nothing. I can swear to that in court, or perhaps — I don't say I can or can't; perhaps I can swear Watson did let you have the money. I spoke to you something about a little plan of mine, by which both of us can make a heap of money. Now, if you will — "

"I know what you are going to say; and I won't have anything to do with your plans."

"Don't be in a hurry, Levi. I can prevent Mr. Watson from coming here. If you will help me through with my little plan, I am your friend, and I will get you out of this scrape. I can do it. If you won't, why, you shall go to the House of Correction as sure as my name is Dock Vincent."

"Well, I wont'!" protested Levi, sturdily. "I would go to the House of Correction for life before I would have anything to do with you or your little plan."

"All right," replied Dock, angrily, as he took his hat, and left the house.

11*

CHAPTER XI.

LEVI'S CHAMBER.

L EVI felt relieved when Dock Vincent had left
him, for it was not pleasant to think that so
vile a man considered him capable of a base and
mean act. He had still no idea of what Dock meant
by his "little plan," except that it was a means of
extorting money from Mr. Watson. The worst he
could conceive of was, that the two who had saved
father and daughter were to present a joint claim
for an increased reward; and this was bad enough to
kindle the young fisherman's indignation. He had
spoken squarely and decidedly, refusing to have anything to do with any "little plan;" and he felt
better after he had done so.

Mr. Gayles had sent a special messenger to Rye
to procure the attendance of Mr. Watson at the examination on the following day, and Levi hoped that

anything Dock and his uncle might say would not
injure him; but he could not help thinking what· an
amount of mischief these two men might do him,
since both of them wished to injure him.

At a later hour in the evening, uncle Nathan, who
had been to Gloucester to recover the money paid
for The Starry Flag, called upon his ward. The old
gentleman was in a very unhappy frame of mind, and,
as may well be supposed, he did not come to con-
dole with the prisoner. He had actually expended
thirty cents in railroad fares, but had not accomplished his purpose. Mr. Hatch declared that he
had given a bill of sale of the Flag, and when
that and the boat were returned to him, he would
restore the money. Mr. Fairfield had spent thirty
cents for nothing, and though his ward would doubtless have to pay it, he was angry at the awful
waste.

"Levi, I've been to Gloucester — paid out thirty
cents," began uncle Nathan, sourly.

"I didn't ask you to go," replied Levi.

"But your carryins on made me go."

"What did you go for?"

"For the money you stole —"

"I didn't steal it," interrupted the prisoner.

"Don't tell me!"

"I shall tell you the truth, and when the time comes I shall prove what I say."

"No matter whether you stole it or not; you ain't a goin to fool away two hundred and fifty dollars on no boat, nor nothin o' that sort — not while I have my senses about me," said the guardian, warmly. "I want you to give me the bill for that boat."

"I haven't got it," replied Levi.

It was in the wallet which he had given to the constable.

"Don't tell me!" exclaimed uncle Nathan, rising from his chair, perhaps surprised that Levi's misfortunes had not yet broken his spirit, and angry at this appearance of opposition. "Mr. Hatch gin you the bill, and I want it."

"I say I haven't got it," repeated Levi. "Do you think I would lie about it?"

"Lie about it! You've told lies enough now to ruin your soul. What have you done with the bill of sale?"

"Mr. Gayles has it."

While uncle Nathan was still raving about the bill, the constable came in, and the irate guardian demanded the important document of him.

"Don't give it to him, Mr. Gayles," said Levi, quietly.

"I have no intention of doing so," added the officer. "This bill may be wanted at the trial, and I shall hold on to it."

"Mr. Gayles, I'm that boy's guardeen, and I want that bill. I want to git back the money the boy stole."

"Perhaps he didn't steal it," quietly suggested Mr. Gayles.

"But he did steal it — don't tell me!"

"When it is proved that he did, it will be my duty to return the boat to Mr. Hatch, and reclaim the money paid for it."

"Have you an idee it won't be proved, Mr. Gayles?" demanded Mr. Fairfield.

"In my opinion Levi will get clear. I don't think he stole the money."

"Who did steal it then?"

"I don't know."

"The money was stole; that boy went off and paid two hundred and fifty dollars for a boat that very morning. Can you put them two things together, Mr. Gayles?"

"They don't prove that Levi stole that money," replied the constable; but he could not help confessing to himself that the boy's position was a trying one.

"Do you believe Ruel Belcher lost any money?" asked Mr. Fairfield.

"I have no doubt he did."

"Then who took it? Nobody got into the house that didn't belong there."

"Levi is going to prove that Mr. Watson let him have the money he paid for the boat. I have sent a man to Rye on purpose for him," added the constable.

"Then who took Ruel's money?" demanded the miser, blankly.

"I think you ought to know better than I," replied Mr. Gayles, with suggestive emphasis.

"Creation! Do you mean to say that I took it?" exclaimed Mr. Fairfield.

"I didn't say so; but I hear that you went into the room where Ruel and Levi slept, after they had gone to sleep."

"I'm that boy's guardeen; I went into the room to git his money, not Ruel's, but I didn't git anything."

"You know best, Mr. Fairfield; but I think you had better not be too hard on the boy."

"Hard on him! I've taken care o' that boy jest as if he'd been my own son. I've looked out for him, and seen to his money, jest as if it was my own, and —"

"That's so," interrupted Levi.

"You see how he treats me fur all I've done for him. Why, he fit me yisterday like a wildcat. I can't do nothin with him, and he must be seen to. I want the boy to behave himself—that's all. Now, he's been stealin."

"Not proved, Mr. Fairfield."

"It's jest as clear to me as the nose on your face." Mr. Gayles had a long nose.

"Perhaps it is. Does Mr. Belcher know what bills Captain Dock paid him?"

"Of course he does; a man like him don't take hundred-dollar bills without lookin at em."

"Very well; Mr. Belcher will swear that he lost bills on a certain bank; if Mr. Hatch swears that he received the same bills from Levi, then a case may be made out against the boy.

"Just so," added uncle Nathan, rather vacantly; and as nothing was to be made by prolonging his visit, he left the house, and went home.

Nathan Fairfield was a miser. Money was his only joy in this world; and he loved it so well that he thought little of the next world. Levi's property amounted to over ten thousand dollars, for the interest more than paid even the exorbitant charges of the guardian for the ward's support. He wanted this money. He had not the patience to think of twelve or fourteen thousand dollars falling into the hands of a young man like Levi, who had "no idee of the vally of money."

Perhaps he did not clearly and distinctly wish that Levi would die; or, if he did, he was not willing to acknowledge as much even to himself; but he could not help thinking how much better it would be if the fortune should come to one who knew how to keep it. With this thought in his mind, where it often was, he entered the kitchen of his home, where Ruel and Mrs. Fairfield were seated.

If the guardian did not allow himself to believe that he wished for the conviction of his ward, it was none the less true that he did wish it. The boy was high-spirited; the House of Correction would break him down; the disgrace might even kill him, and Mr. Fairfield, as the only brother of Levi's deceased father, would inherit his property. What the constable had said about the identity of the bills disturbed him. Levi might escape; if he did he would be more stubborn and disobedient than ever.

"Did you notice the bills that Captain Dock paid you, Ruel?" asked Mr. Fairfield, as he seated himself in a broken chair.

"Of course I did," replied Ruel; and he named the banks by which the bills had been issued. "On one of the hundred-dollar bills there was a great blot of ink, something in the shape of half a star, after the cashier's name, as though the pen had snapped as he finished writing."

12

"Then you'd know the bills if you see 'em?"

"I should know that one, and I think I should the others."

"Bless me! There's another shower comin up!" exclaimed the matron, as a heavy peal of thunder startled her.

The conversation continued for half an hour, when the rain began to fall in torrents. Mrs. Fairfield said the windows in Levi's room were open, and wished her husband to go up and close them. He lighted a lamp and went up stairs for this purpose. As he entered the chamber, the wind began to blow in a fierce squall, as it had in the forenoon of that day. He closed the windows, and was about to descend the stairs, when he heard a sharp rattling in the chimney.

Like everything else about the house, the chimney was in a state of dilapidation. Two or three bricks had been detached by the fierce wind from the top, and had tumbled down the flue into the room. Mr. Fairfield returned to ascertain the extent of the damage, fearful that he might be compelled to employ a mason for a few hours to repair it; and he had paid out so much money for steaks from the "under side of the round" that he felt almost impoverished. The thirty cents he had expended in railroad fares also stung him at that moment.

He pulled down the fireboard, and saw the bricks lying upon the hearth of the large, old-fashioned fireplace. On the top of them lay an object which challenged all his attention, and he forgot the storm, and even the falling chimney.

It was Ruel's wallet!

With eager hand he picked it up. It contained three bills — two one hundreds and a fifty. He was amazed and bewildered by the sight. He examined the bills; on one of them was the blot in the shape of half a star, which Ruel had mentioned. Without a doubt, this was the money his brother-in-law had lost. Levi was innocent — he had not stolen the wallet.

"Husband! what's the matter?" called Mrs. Fairfield, at the foot of the stairs. "What's that noise?"

She had heard the fall of the bricks, and perhaps feared her husband had been struck by them.

"Nothin; only a few bricks fell down chimney,"

replied Mr. Fairfield, hastily thrusting the wallet into his pocket.

He went down stairs, and, having satisfied his wife that the old house had not "caved in," he seated himself in the broken chair again, and, leaving Mrs. Fairfield and her brother to continue their conversation, he proceeded to consider the discovery he had just made.

How came that money in the chimney? It had been concealed there by somebody, and the falling bricks had jostled it from its hiding-place. Who put it there? Not Ruel: he would not hide his own money. He would not cheat himself out of two hundred and fifty dollars. Mr. Fairfield did hot hide it himself. Of course, then, it must have been Levi; no one else could have done it.

Mr. Fairfield was roused from his brown study at half past ten, and reminded that it was time to go to bed. He went to bed. The next morning he took the first train for Gloucester, apparently heedless of the expense, though the thirty cents must have galled him like a thorn in his flesh.

CHAPTER XII.

LEVI MAKES A SPEECH.

HOW a man who has lived threescore years, and stands almost in sight of the open grave, can love money, as Nathan Fairfield loved it, is beyond our comprehension. He had found Ruel's money, for the stealing of which Levi was at least in danger of being sent to the House of Correction. He was entirely satisfied that Levi had stolen the wallet, and concealed it in the chimney; for it was not possible, in his opinion, that any one else could have taken it.

But it was equally clear to him that Levi had not used Ruel's money for the purchase of The Starry Flag. He concluded that the wretched youth had hidden it in the chimney for future use, after the storm, following the loss of the bills, had blown over. It was quite proper that Levi should be convicted,

12*

for he was guilty; and the guardian was determined to "break him down." He actually hated his ward for having a will of his own, and he was determined to have him convicted, if possible.

Mr. Fairfield hastened to the wharf where the boat-builder's shop was located, as soon as the train reached Gloucester. The examination of Levi was to take place at eleven o'clock, and Mr. Hatch had been summoned to appear as a witness; but the guardian found him at the shop.

"Mr. Hatch, I come over to see you agin about that boat business," said Mr. Fairfield, after they had passed the usual salutations. "I want to know sunthin more about it."

"It's bad business; but I hope the boy didn't steal the money," replied the boat-builder.

"I hope he didn't; but I know he did," added the visitor, whose hypocrisy was no match for his malice. "Have you got them bills the boy paid you, Mr. Hatch?"

"I have; I wanted to pay the money away, but I couldn't do it while there was likely to be any trouble about it."

"I wish you'd jest let me look at them bills. I'll give 'em right back to you. Do you know what bank they're on?"

"No, I didn't mind; I only looked at the figures," replied Mr. Hatch, as he took out his pocket-book, and handed the bills to Mr. Fairfield.

"I ruther think I've got a clew to this business," said the guardian, as he took the bills and fumbled in his pocket for his spectacles. "I was talking to my brother-in-law last night about the bills; he looked at 'em, and knows jest what they was."

Mr. Fairfield, with no little agitation and excitement in his manner, put on his spectacles and opened the roll of bills he held in his hand.

"Are those the bills your brother-in-law lost?" asked Mr. Hatch, much interested in the result of the investigation.

"Fact! I don't know's I can tell now; but Ruel knows all about it," replied Mr. Fairfield, as he returned the bills.

"What did you want to see the bills for, if you don't know them when you see them?" asked Mr. Hatch.

"I was comin over to Gloshter this mornin, and I thought I'd jest see you about the bills. I didn't know but you might have paid 'em away; and I wanted you to have 'em with you when you go over to Rockport to the trial."

"It seems to me, Mr. Fairfield, you are very anxious to have your nephew convicted of the crime," added the boat-builder, disgusted at the conduct of the guardian.

"'Tain't so, Mr. Hatch — no sich thing," protested Mr. Fairfield. "You don't understand this business as well as I do. The fact on't is, that money was stole in my house. Ruel more'n half hinted that I stole it myself; and goodness knows, I wouldn't do no sich thing as that."

"But the boy tells where he got the money."

"He don't tell the truth," replied Mr. Fairfield, shaking his head, as he walked away.

Mr. Hatch concluded that the guardian had come to him to assure himself that the identical bills paid for the boat would be produced at the trial. Though he had no respect for the miser, and thought it very unnatural that an uncle should be so forward to have his nephew and ward condemned, he could see no good reason why the whole truth should not come out at the examination. With the bank bills in his pocket-book, he took the same train with Mr. Fairfield for Rockport.

At eleven o'clock Levi was taken to the office of the trial justice by Mr. Gayles. The special messenger who had been sent for Mr. Watson had not yet appeared, but it was believed that the important witness would be present. Mr. Gayles was so confident Levi would be discharged, that no lawyer had been employed to manage his case. The cause was duly brought before the justice, and Ruel Belcher, in his testimony, gave a full history of the loss of his money, as it has been already recited to the reader. Mr. Gayles detailed the arrest, and gave Levi's explanation of the manner he had come into possession of the money with which he had bought the boat; but both Mr. Fairfield and Dock Vincent swore that Levi had told them Mr. Watson gave him no money — had only paid him ten dollars for the fish he had lost.

By this time Mr. Hatch, who had been to see the

minister for whose society he had built the boat, came into the room, and gave his testimony. Ruel had already declared that he could identify the bills he had lost. The boat-builder told what had passed between himself and Levi the day before, which included the statement that Mr. Watson had "let him have" the money.

"Have you the bills the boy paid you?" asked the justice.

"I have," replied Mr. Hatch, taking out his pocket-book and producing the bills.

Ruel was directed to examine them. This appeared to be the turning-point of the case, and those present were breathless with interest. Levi smiled as pleasantly as a summer morning, for he was entirely satisfied that this line of evidence would establish his innocence.

"These are the very bills I lost," said Ruel Belcher.

"What!" exclaimed Levi, springing to his feet, horrified at the words Ruel had spoken.

"Can you swear that those are the bills you lost, Mr. Belcher?" demanded the justice.

"I can."

"How do you identify them?"

"By this blot of ink, in the shape of half a star, near the cashier's signature."

At this stage of the examination the special messenger appeared. He had stopped a moment to do an errand in Gloucester, and had lost the train; but he had no good news for Levi, now overwhelmed by the evidence against him. He had been to Rye, but Mr. Watson had hardly reached the hotel at the beach before he was summoned to Boston by a telegraph despatch to meet some business emergency, and his family had gone with him. The most important witness for Levi, therefore, could not be obtained.

The evidence was all heard. Ruel's money had disappeared; Levi had left his home the next morning without any explanation of his purpose, bought The Starry Flag, and Ruel had identified the bills paid to Mr. Hatch as the money he had lost. Two witnesses had sworn that Levi said Mr. Watson gave him no money. It seemed to be a very plain case, and the justice said as much.

"I know'd just how it would be," said Mr. Fairfield, who sat near Levi.

"I didn't steal that money," cried Levi, springing to his feet again; and he was so overcome by his emotions that the tears streamed down his cheeks. "Mr. Watson let me have that money."

"How could Mr. Watson have given you the very bills which Mr. Belcher lost?" asked the justice, quietly.

"I don't know about that," protested Levi; "but if you will only wait till Mr. Watson comes, he will tell you that he gave me the money."

"That is hardly necessary. The case seems to be made out, and I must commit you for trial. If you wish to ask the witnesses any questions, or offer any new evidence, you may do so."

"I want to ask Mr. Hatch if the bills he showed here are the ones I paid him."

"They are," replied Mr. Hatch.

"Are you sure?" demanded Levi, earnestly. "Have they been out of your hands since I gave them to you?"

"Well, yes — once," answered the boat-builder.

"They have!" exclaimed Levi, catching at this straw.

"Your uncle came over to see me this morning, and wanted to know if I had the same bills you paid me. I told him I had, and showed them to him."

"Did he take them in his hand?"

"He did; but he couldn't tell me whether they were the ones Mr. Belcher had lost or not."

"What did he want to see them for?" asked Levi, greatly excited.

"I don't know."

"I guess you don't!"

Mr. Fairfield was very uneasy and very angry.

"Be calm, Levi, and ask any questions you wish," said the justice.

"Did uncle Nathan give you back the same bills you gave him?"

"I suppose he did; I don't know," replied Mr. Hatch.

"Didn't you examine the bills before you passed them to Mr. Fairfield?" asked the justice.

13

"No, sir; I supposed, of course, he gave me back just what I handed to him."

"May I say something, Squire Saunders?" continued Levi, wiping the tears from his face.

"Anything relating to the matter before us," replied the justice.

"I know I didn't steal that money, Squire Saunders; and I want to have you wait till I can get Mr. Watson here. I've got money enough to send for him. He'll tell you he gave me the money for saving his daughter. I wanted that boat to earn some money with. Here's my uncle; he's my guardian;" and Levi pointed at Mr. Fairfield, who sat squirming like an eel in his chair. "He's meaner than dirt. He don't give me enough to eat, and not much of anything to wear. I want to go to school, and he won't let me. If I should die, he would be the happiest man in Rockport. He wants to break me down! Yes, sir! He wants to break me down! He wants to get rid of me; and he's done everything he could to make it out that I stole this money."

LEVI MAKES A SPEECH IN COURT. Page 146.

"That's a fact!" ejaculated Mr. Hatch, loud enough to be heard by all in the room.

Levi waxed eloquent. He was actually making a speech.

"But I didn't steal it," he continued. "I wouldn't steal any man's money. I've been trying to make something to help myself, because my guardian will not give me what I need. I earned twenty-one dollars, and he tried to take it away from me, Squire Saunders."

"I'm his guardeen!" interposed uncle Nathan, savagely.

"Tell me only about the money, Levi," said the justice.

"He tried to take my money away from me, sir. He wants to make it out that I am a bad boy — that I'm a thief; but I am not. I've been treated worse than a dog, and I won't stand it!"

Levi's tears began to flow again; and as his indignation was kindled at his wrongs, he gesticulated violently, and even shook his fist in the face of his guardian.

"He came into the room where Mr. Belcher and

I slept, night before last, looking for my money — Mr. Belcher told me he did. And he says I stole the money; but I didn't; and I'm almost sure now that he stole it himself!"

Mr. Fairfield jumped up as though he had been shot.

CHAPTER XIII.

MR. HATCH'S TESTIMONY.

YOU villain, you!" gasped Mr. Fairfield, filled with rage at being charged with stealing the money, in addition to the other unpleasant revelations which Levi had made.

"Squire Saunders, I say just what I believe. I don't know as I ought to say it, but I can't help thinking it," added the young fisherman.

"You villain, you! how dare you say I stole the money! I never did sich a thing in my life. I've lived here in Rockport all my days, and I cal'late folks know me well enough to know I wouldn't steal," interposed Mr. Fairfield, a little more composed, when he found himself standing up before the justice and other persons in the room. "It's jest as clear to me as anything in natur can be, that the boy stole that money; and seems to me 'tain't

13 *

exactly right to let him stand here and talk so about one that has been his best friend on airth. I've done everything I could for that boy. I've tried to bring him up right; and to-day he's got more property than he had when his father died. I've done the best I could for him, Squire Saunders, and now you see what I git for't."

Mr. Fairfield, having vented his overcharged feelings, sat down, and looked like a much-abused man.

"Squire Saunders, all I've got to say is, if the money Mr. Hatch showed here is the same that Ruel lost, my uncle must have changed it when he was looking at it, for I know I didn't steal the money. I never touched it, and never saw it," said Levi, stoutly. "All I want is, to have Mr. Watson come here, and tell what he knows about this business."

The prisoner sat down again, with the feeling that he had, at least, raised a doubt in regard to his guilt.

"I am entirely willing to continue the case until Mr. Watson's attendance can be procured," added Squire Saunders; "though, if Mr. Belcher is ready to testify that the money in Mr. Hatch's hands, which he swears was paid to him by Levi, is composed of the identical bills he lost, it is hardly necessary.

Mr. Hatch rose, and seemed much embarrassed.

"I think — that is to say — when I gave my evidence — I hope your honor don't think — I think I was a little too fast," said he, winding up desperately when he found he was making a "mess" of it.

"You wish to correct your testimony?" said the justice, with a smile.

"I said just what I thought was true; but, on second thought, I think I may be mistaken. It didn't occur to me, till Levi·spoke, that the money had been out of my hands."

"You can correct your statements, if you wish," added the magistrate.

"I don't know as I want to correct anything more. When the boy paid me the money, and told me where he got it, so that I was satisfied it was all right, I just looked at the figures on the bills. The national bank bills are all alike to me, and all of 'em good; so I didn't mind much about 'em. I was just going to pay that money away for some lumber I bought, when Mr. Gayles came along to find the boy."

"I thought the proceeds of the sale of the boat were for the benefit of Mr. Ames's church," interposed Squire Saunders.

"Bless you! so they were; but I had money enough in the bank to pay it. I didn't know as I should see the minister for a week or two; so I thought I might as well use the money I had in my pocket to pay for my lumber. It would save me going clear up to the bank, you see."

"No doubt it was all right, Mr. Hatch," added the justice.

"O, it was! you may depend upon it," said the boat-builder, earnestly, — for he was not quite sure that he might not yet be accused of an attempt to purloin from the church the proceeds of the sale; but every one knew that Mr. Hatch would be sunk a thousand feet in the sea rather than wrong any person of the value of one cent. "I might have drawn a check for the lumber; and I should have done so, if I hadn't had that money in my pocket. You see, squire, it would save me taking some steps, and —"

"Never mind that, Mr. Hatch; I am entirely satisfied with your explanation. Confine yourself, if you please, to the matter before the court," interposed the justice.

"Yes, sir. Well, sir, Mr. Gayles came along, and said he was after Levi, because he had stolen the money. I was kind of struck up when I heard this, and didn't think anything more about the lumber. The fact on't is, I haven't paid for it yet; but Mr. Proctor knows I'm good—"

"No doubt you are, Mr. Hatch; but the question relates to the identity of the bills in your possession."

"Just so. Well, sir, Mr. Gayles went off in a boat after Levi, and I didn't hear anything more about the matter till this morning, though I was afraid all of 'em would get cast away when it blowed so yesterday. That was one of the heaviest squalls we have had in these parts since I was a boy. We had another last night, but it wasn't quite so heavy. Well, I was afraid the boats would upset in that squall, and I kept thinking of 'em, for I was out once in a squall, though it wasn't quite so heavy as the one we had yesterday noon; but I've observed

that these squalls coming up from the westward
after such a day — "

" We do not care to listen, just now, to a homily
on meteorology, Mr. Hatch," interrupted the justice;
" you said you didn't look at the bills yesterday."

" No, sir; I didn't say so. I'm on oath, and I
want to tell it just exactly as it was, this time. I
did look at the bills, but only to see the figures.
This morning Mr. Fairfield here came over to see
me about them bills. He wanted to look at 'em,
and I let him have 'em."

" Didn't he change them ? " demanded Levi, impatient under the long speeches of the worthy boat-
builder.

" Bless your soul! I don't know as he did; and,
then again, I don't know *but* he did. I wasn't mind-
ing particularly what he did."

" What did he do when you gave them to him ? "
asked Levi, anxiously; for he was by this time
almost certain that his uncle, when he went into the
room to search for the twenty-one dollars, had stolen
Ruel's wallet, and exchanged the lost bills for those
paid for The Starry Flag.

"Well, he took the bills, and fumbled about his pockets for his spectacles. He found 'em, put 'em on, looked at the bills, and then gave 'em back to me."

"You have no means of knowing whether he changed them or not?" said the justice.

"No, sir; I have not. He might have done it, for all I know."

"Mr. Hatch," continued the magistrate, rather sternly, "are you willing to swear that the bills produced by you in court are the identical ones paid to you by the prisoner?"

"Well, sir, I've told you just exactly how it was; and you can judge for yourself whether the bills are the same ones," replied Mr. Hatch, wiping the perspiration from his brow.

"That is not the point. Mr. Belcher swears positively that the bills you have exhibited are the ones he lost; now, can you swear that they were paid to you by Levi Fairfield?"

"No, sir; I cannot — that is to say, I'm not willing to do so. I'll swear to anything in reason, but — "

"Can you swear that Mr. Fairfield did change the bills?" added Squire Saunders.

"No, I certainly cannot. He might have changed 'em, but you see I don't know whether he did or not."

"That will do, Mr. Hatch; sit down, if you please," continued the justice. "Mr. Belcher, do you wish to make any change in your testimony?"

"No, sir; I don't know that I do."

"You are quite positive the bills produced by Mr. Hatch are the identical ones you lost?"

"I'm just as sure of it as I am that I stand here," replied Ruel, confidently. "I looked them over very carefully, for I'm not much used to handling hundred-dollar bills, and I rather liked the looks of them."

"Where did you get the bills?"

"They were paid to me yesterday by Captain Vincent."

"I think I should know them again," added Dock, who was then invited to examine them. "They are the very bills I paid Mr. Belcher," — he did not say how reluctantly. "This new one was given me by Mr. Watson."

"Mr. Fairfield, do you wish to alter your evidence?" said Squire Saunders, turning to Levi's guardian.

"Not one word on't!" replied he, with energy.

"You visited the chamber in which Mr. Belcher and Levi were asleep — did you not?"

"Yes, sir; I did go in. The fact on't is, that boy had twenty-one dollars, and I'm his guardeen."

"We know that," interposed the justice, tartly.

"He's gettin to be a bad boy, and it's high time sunthin' was done. He's got to be seen to, or —"

"What did you go into the room for?"

"To git Levi's money. I didn't want to have him fool it away, waste the money, and hurt himself."

"Did you find his money?"

"No, I did not; I wish I had."

"You found no money?"

"Not a cent."

"For what purpose did you visit Gloucester this morning?"

"To see Mr. Hatch. You see, I was afraid he'd pay away them bills —"

14

"And your nephew would not be convicted," added the justice, with evident disgust.

"If that boy stole the money — and I know he did — I want the facts to come out jest as they be. He's a bad boy, and he's gittin wus every day. I can't do nothin with him; he fit me like a wildcat; and it's a good deal better to have him seen to afore it's too late, than tis to let him go to ruin, and then try to save him from the error of his ways. I b'lieve in shettin the door afore the hoss is stole."

"Did you change the bills handed to you by Mr. Hatch?"

"Did I change 'em!" repeated Nathan Fairfield, trying to look savage and indignant; but the attempt was a miserable failure, for his emphasis was broken-backed, and his thin lips quivered. "Did I change 'em! You've known me a good many years, Squire Saunders — "

"Answer the question."

"Of course I didn't change 'em. What should *I* change 'em for? I only wanted to be sure that Mr. Hatch didn't pass them bills off."

"That is sufficient," said the justice, turning to Levi, whom he called up. "Levi, this is not a court to try you for the crime with which you are charged. It is my duty to examine the evidence for and against you, and determine whether there are sufficient grounds for holding you to answer in the proper court on the charge against you. This is not your trial."

"I know it, sir," replied Levi; "I'm ready to do whatever you say, but I didn't steal that money any more than you did."

"Understand me, Levi: I do not say you are guilty, but there is probable cause for believing you guilty, as the case stands at present."

"It wouldn't stand so if Mr. Watson had been here," added Levi.

"As you seem to lay a great deal of stress upon the appearance of Mr. Watson, I will, if you desire, continue the case for a few days."

"I do desire it," replied Levi, decidedly.

"Very well; I will put the case off for one week; but in the mean time I must commit you, unless you offer sufficient bail for your appearance. Perhaps your uncle would be your bail."

"I'm willin to do anything in reason, squire; but that boy would be jest as sartin to run away as he would be to eat when he's hungry," interrupted Mr. Fairfield.

"If he could get something to eat," added Levi, bitterly.

Very much to the prisoner's surprise, a Cape Ann *millionnaire* — worth one hundred and fifty thousand dollars — came forward, and offered to "go bail" for him. The father-in-law of Mr. Gayles also offered himself, both gentlemen having been secured by the grateful constable. The bail was acceptable, and Levi left the office, to appear again in one week.

CHAPTER XIV.

AFTER THE EXAMINATION.

OF those who attended the examination of Levi, one half believed that Mr. Fairfield had stolen the money, and the other half that Levi was guilty of the theft. Some thought that Levi was a bad boy; and all knew that his uncle was a hard and mean man.

The prisoner left the office with Mr. Gayles. The boat-builder was in great trouble. He was now entirely satisfied that the money in his possession was that which had been stolen from Ruel Belcher; and when the squire told him he might restore it to owner, taking his receipt therefor, he made haste to get rid of it.

"Now you have got your money, Mr. Belcher, and you ought to be satisfied," said he, as he gave up the bills.

14*

"I am entirely satisfied."

"Now, do you believe that boy stole the money?"

"Sartin he did," interposed Mr. Fairfield. "Nobody else could have took it."

"I don't say you took it, Mr. Fairfield; but I can't quite get it through my head that Levi isn't an honest boy," added Mr. Hatch.

"The fact on't is, I know the boy stole the money. Mr. Watson didn't give him no two hundred and fifty dollars for haulin that gal into the dory," continued Mr. Fairfield. "He's a rich man; and he didn't git rich foolin away his money in that shape. It stands to reason a man like him wouldn't do no sich thing."

"If Mr. Watson did give him two hundred and fifty dollars, where is it now? That's the question," suggested Ruel Belcher. "I'm just as sure this money paid me by Mr. Hatch is what I lost, as I am that I stand here now."

"I don't believe Mr. Watson give him any money; if he did, the boy has hid it," said the guardian.

"I think we'd better hunt round, and see if we can't find it," added Ruel.

"Levi seemed to be very sure that Mr. Fairfield changed the bills when he looked at them this morning," continued Squire Saunders, glancing at the guardian.

"That boy hates me, and all because I've tried to do well by him, and make a man of him. He'd say anything," replied Mr. Fairfield; but he did not like the look which the magistrate gave him.

The conversation continued for some time longer, but without making any of the party wiser than they were before. Mr. Fairfield was disturbed and uneasy. He wanted to get away, but he didn't wish to leave while it was possible that anything might be said to implicate him. He knew that he had, at that moment, the identical bills in his pocket which Mr. Watson had paid Levi; he knew that he had changed the bills in the morning, during his interview with the boat-builder; and he was afraid — as all guilty men are — that some circumstance might betray him.

But we must do the guardian the justice to say, that he believed Levi had stolen Ruel's wallet. He had found it concealed in the chimney. He was con-

fident that no one but the boy could have stolen it.
He did not steal it himself—he knew that; and Ruel
would not purloin his own money. If he did steal
it—and he did—he ought to be convicted; and the
fact that the wallet had been found in the chimney,
would be as likely to convict the uncle as the
nephew.

Ruel and Mr. Fairfield left the office together;
but they soon separated, and Nathan went home
alone. He was very nervous, for he had done a
mean, base, and wicked act, though this did not
trouble him half so much as the fear that what
he had done would be discovered. Mr. Watson
might come to Rockport within a few days. Probably he would be able to identify the large bills he
had given to Levi. What if they should be found
upon him? The cold sweat started on his forehead at the very thought, for it would prove that
he had changed the bills Mr. Hatch handed to
him.

He was alarmed. He reached his dilapidated mansion, and went in. Though he told his wife the
result of the examination, he was not disposed to

enlarge upon the subject. What if the constable should come to look for the bills? He was terrified as the thought flashed through his mind, and jumping out of his chair, he went up stairs to Levi's room. Taking the stolen wallet from his pocket, he placed the bills he had taken from Mr. Hatch just as he found the original contents when the wallet fell out of its hiding-place.

Without thinking that he was attired in his best clothes, he crawled into the fireplace, and then thrust his head up into the capacious flue. It was an old-fashioned house, and the fireplaces were large enough to hold from a foot to half a cord of wood. Mr. Fairfield was looking for a safe place for the wallet. He intended to restore it to the chimney where he had found it, until the excitement had subsided, when the money could be used. But if he put it where it was before, Levi, who had concealed it, would find it again, and, before the week had expired, would take it, and leave for parts unknown.

Mr. Fairfield concluded to place it about eight feet above the hearth, where he found a projecting brick upon which it could rest. Levi, not finding the wallet where he had hidden it, would naturally conclude that it was gone, and not search higher up for it. At the same time, if Levi should be driven to confess the theft, and reveal the hiding-place of the wallet, then it would be found in the chimney. But he hoped the boy would not be weak enough to confess; and when the trouble was all over, Mr. Fairfield could put the money in his pocket.

The miserable old wretch was satisfied with the precautions he had used, and was reasonably confident that his own villany would not be discovered. He had hardly put up the fireboard when he heard a very emphatic knocking at the front door. Hastening down stairs, he found that Mrs. Fairfield had just admitted Mr. Hatch and the constable, who were attended by Levi.

When the party at the office separated, Mr. Hatch had gone directly to Mr. Gayles's house. He was a little anxious about the boat, and wished to settle the question in regard to the present ownership of The Starry Flag. He told Levi that he had given up the money which Ruel had identified as his own.

"But, Levi, you have the bill of sale of the boat," he added.

"I won't keep it, Mr. Hatch; I'll give it back to you," said Levi. "I suppose, as things have turned out, The Starry Flag don't belong to me any longer."

"Well, I've given back the money, and I think I ought to have the boat again."

"You can take her, sir," replied Levi, sadly. "She lies in the cove; or, if you wish, I'll sail her back to Gloucester for you."

"Well, I don't know," added Mr. Hatch, scratching his head violently in his perplexity. "Bad as matters look, some how or other, I can't help thinking things will come out right in the end."

"I know they will; but I don't see that I am likely to have the boat; and you may as well take her now as at any other time," answered Levi, gloomily — for the bright visions of owning and sailing the beautiful boat had passed away. "I believe my uncle stole that money, and laid it to me. I'm pretty certain he changed the bills when you let him have them this morning."

"Then, of course, he has those you paid to Mr. Hatch," said the constable.

"I'm almost sure he has."

"Do you know them, Levi?"

"I'll bet I do! I studied them well," replied the young fisherman, eagerly. "All three of them were on the same bank, and they were new and stiff."

"Those I had in court were on three different banks, but one of them was a new one," added the constable.

"Yes; and that new one was on the same bank as mine — the Continental National Bank, Boston. I saw it when Ruel looked at them. I'll bet the hundred-dollar bill was the one paid by Mr. Watson to Dock Vincent."

"I've a great mind to get out a search warrant, and see what money the old skinflint has on hand," continued Mr. Gayles.

Mr. Hatch thought he would be willing to show his money, if everything was right with him, and thus remove all suspicion against him.

"We can go down and see him, at any rate," he added.

"I will go with you, for I want to show you where The Stary Flag lies," said Levi.

"About the boat, I don't know as I'll take her round with me, Levi. On the whole, I guess I won't," continued Mr. Hatch; "I can't help thinking that things will come out right."

"I know they will, Mr. Hatch," answered Levi, decidedly; for however dark the prospect looked, he did not at any time lose his faith in the future.

"I'll tell you what I'll do, Levi," continued Mr. Hatch; "I'll leave the boat in your care till this business is settled up. You will use her carefully; and Mr. Gayles can have an eye to her, if there's any trouble."

"Thank you, sir! I'm very much obliged to you, Mr. Hatch. I'd like to use her; but I don't much think I shall ever own her now," said Levi: "uncle Nathan has got the money I ought to pay for her."

"Mr. Watson must come here in a few days," added Mr. Gayles. "Now we will go and see what we can make of Mr. Fairfield."

The party arrived at the house of the miser, after paying a visit to The Starry Flag at the cove.

15

They were ushered into the kitchen by Mrs. Fair-field.

"Massy sakes! Where *hev* you been, Nathan?" cried the matron, as her husband, begrimed from head to foot with dust, ashes, and soot, presented himself at the door. "What on airth hev you been doin?"

"I hain't been doin nothin," replied Mr. Fairfield, to whom his wife's words sounded like an accusation.

He had evidently rubbed his hand across his face, after it was thoroughly "smooched" with soot, and he looked very much like the driver of a charcoal cart. The visitors, in spite of the seriousness of the occasion, could not restrain their laughter. Mr. Fair-field tried to laugh, making a very painful effort to do so, which caused him to look all the more comical.

"What *hev* you been doin?" repeated his wife.

"I've been fixin that chimbly that blowed over last night," replied Mr. Fairfield, finding it necessary to explain his sooty aspect.

"With your best clothes on, Nathan Fairfield!" exclaimed his careful spouse.

"I didn't think of that," he replied, now astonished at his own recklessness in the use of his best clothes.

Mr. Gayles then explained that, in order to remove all suspicion, Mr. Fairfield had better exhibit what money he had on hand.

"Sartin; I'm glad you've come. I'll show you every dollar of money I've got in the house," replied the miser, with sudden energy, as he took out his pocket-book, and handed it to the officer.

Of course the bills which Mr. Watson had paid to Levi were not to be found in his pocket-book, or in the bureau, where he kept his spare funds.

"I hope you are satisfied now," said Mr. Fairfield, in a tone as triumphant as the speaker could make it.

"The bills don't seem to be about you, or in your bureau," replied Mr. Gayles.

"I think we had better look into that chimney," suggested Levi.

Mr. Fairfield turned pale, and the black "smooches" on his face looked blacker than before by the contrast.

CHAPTER XV.

LEVI EXPLORES THE CHIMNEY.

MR. FAIRFIELD was appalled when Levi suggested that the chimney should be examined. He was very certain that his ward had stolen the wallet and hidden it, and Levi was just as certain that his uncle was guilty of the crime. To the guardian it made but little difference who stole the money, for if the wallet were found in the chimney, it would be lost to him when the storm had blown over.

"What do you want to look into the chimbly for?" demanded he, when the constable exhibited a readiness to adopt Levi's suggestion.

"We may find the money there," replied Mr. Gayles.

"I begin to see into this business a little grain," added Mr. Fairfield; "and I ain't a goin to have you ransackin my house for nothin. Have you got a sarch-warrant?"

"No; I have not," answered the officer of the law.

"Then you can't go no further," said the miser, decidedly; for he knew very well that the search in the chimney would be sure to involve him in trouble.

"I will procure a search-warrant, if you are not willing I should make the examination without one."

"Well, I ain't willin."

"If you are an innocent man, Mr. Fairfield, I suppose the search would do you more good than harm. It's a fact that about one half the people in town believe you stole Ruel's money."

"They no business to think so," protested the miser. "I'm an innocent man. Do you think I'd steal my brother-in-law's money?"

"You can see through a mill-stone when there's a hole in it, Mr. Fairfield."

"I reckon I can; and I see through this mill-stone, too. You've got that boy; and you don't know as well as I do what a bad boy he is. He stole that money — don't tell me — I know he did

15 *

Now he wants to look up chimbly — don't he? What does all that mean? He stole the money, and he hid it somewhere in the chimbly, for 's all I know. Now he wants to let you find it, and make it out that I hid it. He's a bad boy, and it don't look right for you to hear to him, and not mind a word that I say," continued Mr. Fairfield.

"Uncle Nathan, I'd like to know what you've been poking in the chimney for, the first thing after the court, with your best clothes on?" inquired Levi, in a very pointed manner.

"Don't I tell you the top of the chimbly blowed in last night in the squall, and I've been fixin it?" snarled the uncle. "Mr. Gayles, that boy said I stole the money; yes, he said so in the court, and I'm goin to make him prove it."

"I think I can prove it before we get through with this business," said Levi.

"Well, you ain't goin pokin about my house no more, not without you have a sarch-warrant," added uncle Nathan, very decidedly.

"Don't you think you had better let Mr. Gayles look up that chimney?" interposed Mr. Hatch.

"I don't think no such thing, and I ain't agoin to do it."

"Just as you say, Mr. Fairfield."

"I know it's just as I say. Levi stole the money, and hid it. If he's a mind to confess that he stole it, and says it is in the chimbly, I'm willing to let you look there."

"I didn't steal the money, and I didn't hide it, and I'm not going to confess it," said Levi, emphatically.

Mr. Fairfield positively refused to permit the chimney to be searched, unless the officer was armed with the proper authority to do so, and the party left the house to procure the warrant; but Levi determined to remain near the house, and observe the movements of his uncle, who was not the man to spoil his best clothes by exploring the interior of a chimney, unless for some extraordinary reason. He was quite sure that Mr. Fairfield had changed the bills which Mr. Hatch showed him, and he was equally confident that the two hundred and fifty dollars paid him by Mr. Watson was somewhere in the house. His uncle's sooty appearance suggested the hiding-place ; and, warrant or no warrant, he was determined to discover whether or not the money was hidden in the chimney. Without inform-ing Mr. Gayles of his purpose, he returned to his uncle's house.

"What do you want now?" demanded uncle Na-than, as he entered the kitchen.

"I want my old clothes," replied Levi; "I'm going a fishing."

"You ain't goin up stairs, no how," interposed Mr. Fairfield. "You villain, you! You want to make it out that I stole the money — do you? You've hid it somewhere, and you want to put it in a place where the constable will find it, and lay it to me. I know you, you villain, you!"

"I want my old clothes."

"Git 'em for him, wife. If he put that money in the chimbly, I mean to have the officer find it just where he put it. I ain't a goin to have things fixed so as to git me into trouble."

Mrs. Fairfield brought the old clothes down from the chamber, and Levi went into the wood-shed to change his dress. It was clear that his uncle would not permit him to enter his own room, and he was very anxious to examine the interior of the chimney before his guardian had an opportunity to remove the stolen wallet. When he had put on his old clothes, he went out doors, and looked up at the broken chimney top. He was a "born sailor," nimble as a cat, and dizzy heights had no terrors for him. Springing to the roof of the shed first, and then to the top of the house, whose half-decayed shingles rattled and snapped beneath his feet, he reached the top of the chimney. It was spacious enough even at the outlet to permit his passage down.

Bracing his knees against the sides, and using such projecting bricks as afforded him a foothold, he gradually descended the flue till he reached the fireplace in his own chamber. Removing the fireboard so as to give him more light, he carefully examined the inside of the chimney; but the wallet was not to be found.

While he was changing his clothes in the woodshed, Mr. Fairfield had removed it again, and concealed it in another place. The miser had promptly concluded that the finding of the wallet in its original hiding-place would be of more damage to him than it would to Levi, especially as he had been seen, so soon after the examination, covered with soot.

Levi was disappointed. His uncle had outwitted him, though of course the young man did not know it. He was reasonably certain that his guardian had the money, but he could prove nothing. He returned through the flue to the roof of the house, and made his way down to the solid earth again. It is quite probable that his uncle knew what he was about, but he said nothing.

Squire Saunders declined to issue a search-warrant for the purpose indicated by Mr. Gayles. The law requires that the object to be searched for shall be particularly designated. The bills which Ruel Belcher had lost had been identified and restored to the owner; and it did not appear that any other bills had been lost. Nothing could be done, therefore, but wait for the time to which the examination of Levi had been postponed. On the following day Mr. Gayles went to Boston, and found Mr. Watson, who was deeply interested in the welfare of the young fisherman, and promised to be present at the examination.

"I would go down to Rockport and stay two or three weeks, if there was a decent place to bathe," said Mr. Watson, as the constable was leaving his counting-room.

"There isn't a better place on the coast," replied Mr. Gayles, emphatically.

"I won't trust my daughter on those rocks again. She is so fond of the salt water, that she must be in it, if she is near the shore."

"There isn't a better place in the world than Back Beach, in our town," added Mr. Gayles.

"But that is a mile from Pigeon Cove."

"Well, you can board down in the village, within a stone's throw of the beach. Mr. Babson has two nice rooms in a new house, and his folks will take first-rate care of you."

Mr. Watson liked the idea, and instructed the constable to engage the rooms for him, and fit up a bathing-room on Back Beach for the use of his family. On the Saturday afternoon following, he took possession of his apartments at Mr. Babson's. Two little rooms under the public hall, which extended nearly down to high-water mark, had been fitted up for dressing-rooms, and before evening Bessie Watson and her father were again floundering in the brine. The little water-nymph was delighted with the place, the beach was so hard, the water so clear, and the billows so long and gentle.

While the little maiden and her father were sporting in the waves, The Starry Flag, with all sail spread to the gentle breeze, glided up as near to the shore as the depth of water would permit. Levi lived in the boat now. He would not go to his uncle's house, and had slept two nights in the cuddy forward. Mr. Watson and his daughter were ex-pected, and he had run down to see them. When they came out of the water, he took them on board at Old Pier.

"Levi, I'm glad to see you," said Mr. Watson, as he stepped into the boat ; "and Bessie thinks you are a hero of the first water."

"Salt water, father," laughed Bessie.

"Thank you, sir. I would have given more to see

you last Thursday than any other man in the world," replied Levi.

"I'm sorry you have had so much trouble, Levi, about this boat," added Mr. Watson. "But I see you keep The Starry Flag."

"The owner lent her to me. I gave him back the bill of sale. I don't own her now."

"But you shall own her, if she costs me a thousand dollars. Mr. Gayles told me about this affair. Do you really think your uncle changed the bills when Mr. Hatch let him look at them?"

"I know very well that I paid Mr. Hatch the money you lent me. I didn't steal Ruel's wallet, and there is only one other person that could have done it."

"You mean your uncle."

"Yes, sir; he has never treated me well, and he wants to break me down. I believe he has the bills now which you gave me, and I mean to keep watch of him till I find them."

"Be prudent, Levi, and it will come out right," added Mr. Watson.

The Starry Flag stood out as far as Half Tide

Rock, and then returned. The merchant and his daughter were delighted with the boat, and promised themselves much pleasure in sailing and fishing in her.

"There comes the Griffin," said Levi, as the Flag was approaching the Old Pier.

"What's the Griffin?"

"She is Dock Vincent's schooner. He is the man who picked you up the other day."

The Griffin came to anchor, and Levi, as he landed his passengers, could not help thinking about her skipper's "little plan," and wondering whether the present visit of the merchant and his daughter would not bring trouble to one or the other of them.

CHAPTER XVI.

ON MIKE'S POINT.

MR. FAIRFIELD was the most miserable man on Cape Ann. Even the absence of Levi, though it saved the provisions necessary to satisfy the voracious appetite of a boy of fifteen, worried him intensely. He could not help believing that the young fisherman, during this time, was plotting and conspiring against him; that he was setting awful traps, into which, with all his shrewdness and worldly policy, he might fall, losing his reputation, and, what was worse, his money. He wished the boy would stay at home, or at least come home nights, so that he could keep the run of him.

The miser had changed the bills handed to him by the boat-builder — he knew what others only suspected. He was fearful that he had slightly overdone his part, and that in his efforts to cover up the wrong which he had actually committed, he should prove himself to be guilty of what he had not done.

But his chances were still good, in his own estimation, harassed though he was by doubts and fears. It could not be proved that he changed the bills. Mr. Watson might swear that he had given Levi the money to buy the boat, but that would not prove that he had not stolen Ruel's money. If worse came to worst, and he found himself compelled to sacrifice the two hundred and fifty dollars, he could place the wallet in a locker in The Starry Flag, or in some other place, which would fasten the guilt upon the boy. The case was by no means hopeless, though it did not work as well as the miser had hoped and expected. ·

Levi had a powerful friend in Mr. Watson. He was a man of wealth and influence, and this fact troubled Mr. Fairfield. The accused would be ably defended at the examination, which was yet to take place. Probably there would be smart lawyers employed, who would indulge in ugly cross-examinations, and dig down into the deepest depths of human nature. It gave him a cold sweat to think of the awkward questions he would be asked, and of the efforts which would be made to induce him to contradict himself. But if the case looked desperate on the day before the examination, he could easily change the whole aspect of it by carrying out the policy he had adopted when he found the wallet in the chimney. Mr. Fairfield still believed that Levi would be committed for trial, and that he should be able to keep the money himself.

Dock Vincent had delivered his cargo of fish in Boston, and returned to Rockport, where he expected to obtain another freight the following week. As Levi left Old Pier, after landing his passengers, he passed near the Griffin. He was sorry to see Dock come back, now that Mr. Watson had returned. He was afraid the grasping villain would make a demand upon the merchant for a larger reward, and perhaps mention his name. Dock was a mean man, and capable of doing very mean things. As the Flag stood away from the shore, Levi almost made up his mind to say something to Mr. Watson about the "little plan," and put him on his guard against the extortion of the wretch; but, as it might look like a hint,

16 *

. or at least open the question as to whether the merchant had sufficiently rewarded those who saved his
daughter and himself, he decided to say nothing about
the matter.   •

Levi stood out from the shore to the deep water,
where his boat could float at low tide, and came to
anchor there.   After furling his sails, it was nearly
dark, and he concluded to "pipe to supper." He had
laid in a stock of provisions, consisting of a small
boiled ham, bread, cakes, and pies. He had no facilities for making tea or coffee, though he had heard
of an apparatus for making coffee with a spirit lamp,
which he intended to procure; but he had a breaker
of water on board, with whose contents he was satisfied for the present.

The young fisherman, without being an epicure,
was very fond of good living; and certainly his fare
on board the boat was much better than that to
which he had been accustomed at the house of his
miserly uncle; and, what filled the measure of his
satisfaction, there was plenty of it. Levi supped like
a prince, and having cleared away his table, — which
was a swinging board in the cuddy, — he sat for an

hour watching the undulating sea as The Starry
Flag gently rose and fell on the long, regular billows, and listening to their dull roar as they broke
upon the beaches and the rocks.

Then he thought of the coming examination, of
the triumph which awaited him when Mr. Watson
gave his evidence, for he believed that he would fully
establish his innocence. The darkness gathered around
him, and it was time to pipe below. He had not
yet purchased the mattresses for the bunks of his
boat, but he had made up a bed of old clothes in
one of them, using the tattered sail of the dingy
dory for a covering. If he ate like a prince, he slept
better than princes are traditionally said to sleep, for
he did not wake till daylight.

It was Sunday, and, as he had procured all his clothes
from his uncle's, he dressed himself in his best, after
he had washed down the boat and put her in order.
He had declined an offer of ten dollars to take a
party out to the fishing-grounds on that day, and
running in at Old Pier, he went to church and to
Sunday school as usual.

The next morning he went after dog-fish, and pro-

cured a full cargo, whose livers added ten dollars to
the funds in his exchequer. By three o'clock in the
afternoon he had sold his fare to Mr. Gayles, and
washed up the boat, so that she was as clean and
sweet as a lady's barge. He intended to devote the
rest of the day to a pleasure-trip to Thatcher's Island.
The occasion was to be complimentary to Bessie
Watson. He had spoken of the trip on Saturday
night, and Mr. Watson had consented, for he had
perfect confidence in Levi's prudence, as well as his
seamanship. Mrs. Watson had been invited, but she
was always so sick that sailing parties afforded her
no pleasure, and she declined to go. In order to
make the occasion more agreeable to Bessie, Levi
had invited Estelle Haskell, Annie Rowe, Jenny
Robarts, John Marshall, and Charley Manning, to
join the party.

Levi always did "the handsome thing;" and though
it was, perhaps, rather extravagant, he expended three
dollars and a half in the purchase of the nicest cake
the confectioners made, and in fruit and iced lemonade. All the party except Bessie Watson were at
Old Pier, the place appointed, at four o'clock. But

where was the bright, particular star of the occasion? She did not come. Charley Manning volunteered to go up to Mr. Babson's and inform her that the company were waiting for her.

"She has gone down to Central Wharf," said Charley, when he returned, breathless with the haste he had used. "She thought that was the place where we were to go on board."

"All right: there is a good breeze, and we can run round there in fifteen minutes," replied Levi, as he cast off from the wharf, and hoisted the jib.

"But she may get tired of waiting," said Jenny Robarts; "she must have been there half an hour now."

"There is Charley Parsons on the wharf; he will run over and tell her to wait till we come," suggested Estelle.

Charley Parsons was a good fellow, and readily promised to do Levi this favor, especially as he was invited to join the party. The Starry Flag stood out of the dock, and as the wind was west, he was obliged to stand over towards Knowlton's Wharf, in order to get a "slant" which would carry him clear

of the high wall that protected the docks from storms.
This course carried him close to the Griffin, which
still lay at anchor in the bay. As The Starry Flag
passed her, Levi saw Dock Vincent put off from her
in a boat, and pull towards Mike's Point. There
was plenty of wind, though it was not heavy enough
to make the proposed trip uncomfortable, and the
Flag soon disappeared beyond the high wall.

Charley Parsons, who had been commissioned to
see Bessie, was a good boy; and as he had been
invited to go with the party, he thought it proper
on his way to run home and tell his mother that
he was going. When he reached Central Wharf,
where he expected to find Bessie, she was not
there.

The fair young lady from the city was very fond
of the salt water, as we have already more than
hinted, and she was especially delighted with sailing. With childish impatience she had hastened to
the wharf at which she had understood the party
was to embark, half an hour before the appointed
time. She had nearly exhausted her patience when
she heard the clock strike four. The Starry Flag

was not at the wharf, and was not to be seen inside of the breakwater. Then she inquired of a man who was packing fish where she was. He had just seen the Flag at Old Pier, and he told her so.

Satisfied that some mistake had been made, she hastened to the wharf indicated, and reached the head of the pier just in time to see the boat standing over towards Knowlton's Wharf. Believing that she could hail her from Mike's Point, she ran with all her might, and did not stop to breathe till she stood on the jagged rocks which formed the headland. But The Starry Flag had gone about on the other tack, and was now half way over to the great breakwater, Charley Parsons had missed Bessie by going to his home before he delivered his message.

Just as Bessie reached the rocks on Mike's Point, Dock Vincent landed from his boat, and making his way up to the place where she stood, immediately recognized her.

"Ah, Miss Bessie," said he.

"O, Mr. Dock, I am so tired and so disappointed!" gasped she, exhausted with running.

"Why, what is the matter, miss?"

Bessie explained what the matter was.

"O, well, if that is all, Miss Bessie, I can soon make it all right," replied Dock.

There was something about the skipper of the Griffin that the little maiden did not like. He was an evil-looking man, and though he had rendered her father and herself a great service, she did not feel like trusting him, and she instinctively shrank from him.

"What can you do for me?" she asked, timidly.

"Get into my boat, and I will pull off and put you on board of The Starry Flag," answered Dock.

"But you can't catch her."

"She will come about in a moment, and stand over this way again."

"I think I will wait here, then," added she, for she had not the courage to go in a boat with such an evil man; and the instinct of self-preservation seemed to require her to refuse — the instinct which Heaven gives to the virtuous and the innocent.

Dock tried to persuade her, but she was timidly firm, and refused to go.

"I won't hurt you," said he, rather rudely.

ON MIKE'S POINT. Page 193.

"I think I will wait here, Mr. Dock."

"I think you won't," said he, suddenly laying hold of her, and taking her up in his arms like a child.

Bessie tried to scream, but her voice failed her. She attempted to escape, but Dock was a powerful man, and held her as easily as he would have held a baby, and bore her down the rocks towards his boat.

This was part of his "little plan."

17

CHAPTER XVII.

THE EVIL MAN.

BESSIE WATSON was paralyzed with terror at the violence of the evil man. She found it impossible to struggle, or even to utter a scream. The rocks were rough, and the passage to the water difficult and dangerous; but Dock threaded his way in safety over the slippery boulders to the boat, in the stern-sheets of which he deposited his burden.

"Don't be frightened, Miss Bessie," said he, in tones as soothing as his rough nature could command. "I won't hurt you if you keep still and behave yourself."

"Let me go — do, Mr. Dock," pleaded she, when she could find voice for utterance.

"Keep still where you be, and I won't hurt you," replied Dock, as he hauled in the painter, and pushed off the boat.

"What are you going to do with me, Mr. Dock?"

"No matter now what I'm going to do. After I've done as much for anybody as I have for you, I don't like to be insulted."

"Insulted! O, Mr. Dock, what have I done?" moaned Bessie, alarmed by the words of her terrible captor.

"You wouldn't trust me, even after I have saved your life, and your father's, too. I offered to put you on board of The Starry Flag, and you wouldn't let me do it. That was an insult."

"I didn't mean it, Mr. Dock — indeed I didn't!"

"No matter what you meant; you insulted me. I won't hurt you if you keep still and mind what I say. But if you attempt to holler, or make any signs, I'll stuff my handkerchief in your mouth, and tie you hand and foot."

"You will not be so cruel, Mr. Dock. I am frightened almost to death. Do let me go back to my mother."

"Don't whine; I tell you I won't hurt you."

"But what are you going to do with me?"

"I'm only going to put you on board of The

Starry Flag, with Levi. Now, shut up, and don't
say another word," answered Dock, shipping his oars,
and pulling the boat round.

Bessie hoped the evil man would do what he said
he would, but her fears were stronger than her
hopes; and, as she sat in the boat, her delicate
frame trembled. Dock pulled towards the Griffin,
and as the boat receded from the shore, Bessie discovered The Starry Flag beyond the high wall, by
Old Pier.

"You *will* put me into The Starry Flag — won't
you?" said she, rising from her seat, and watching
the beautiful sail-boat, as she glided swiftly on her
course.

"Of course I will. Sit down and keep still," replied Dock, gruffly.

"I will be ever so much obliged to you if you
will; and I will do anything for you!" exclaimed
Bessie, earnestly.

"You are very willing to trust me now," sneered
Dock.

"I will trust you now, Mr. Dock. I didn't mean
any harm, and I wouldn't insult you for all the world."

"Perhaps you wouldn't now."

In a few moments the boat was within hail of the Griffin, on whose deck were two men watching them.

"Shake out the mainsail, and hoist it!" shouted Dock to his little crew.

"What are you going to do?" asked Bessie, terrified anew by this ominous order.

"I am going round to Gloucester to-night," he replied.

"But you were going ashore when you met me."

"I have changed my mind."

"And you are not rowing towards The Starry Flag now," added the fair prisoner, beginning to lose all hope again.

"I can't catch the sail-boat with a pair of oars," answered Dock, as the boat came up alongside the Griffin. "Now, jump aboard my vessel."

"I don't want to," pleaded Bessie.

"It don't make any difference whether you want to or not — you will. Come, be lively!"

"You will put me on board of The Starry Flag — won't you, Mr. Dock?"

17 *

"Of course I will. Don't I tell you I'm going round to Gloucester? I'll run in by the breakwater, and hail the Flag. What are you afraid of?"

Bessie could hardly tell what she was afraid of. Dock Vincent's plan certainly seemed to be a good one, and he appeared to be carrying it out in good faith. Her common sense assured her that it would be impossible to overtake a swift-sailing craft, like The Starry Flag, in a row-boat. But though it all looked right, and Dock promised fairly, the tones and the manner of the evil man were all against him, and, try as hard as she could to trust him, she found it utterly impossible to do so.

"Come, I'll help you on board," said the skipper, as he took her by the arm, and led her to the vessel's side.

His touch, in spite of herself, seemed to thrill her with horror. He was a terrible man to her, but she could not resist him. With Dock's assistance, she climbed over the rail, and reached the deck of the schooner, whither she was followed by her captor, when he had secured the boat.

"Now, you may go down into the cabin, and stay

there till I call you," continued Dock, pointing to the companion-way.

"I don't want to go down; I'll stay on deck, if you please," replied Bessie.

"But I don't please, and you must go down into the cabin," added the skipper, rudely. "You are in the way on deck, and if you should get knocked overboard by the swinging of a boom, what would your father say to me?"

"O, I will be very careful, Mr. Dock; and really there is no danger of my being knocked overboard. Don't make me go into the cabin, if you please. I like to look at the water, and the waves, and the vessels."

"I don't want to put my hands on you again, but if you don't go below I shall have to do so."

Bessie looked up into his ugly face. There was an expression of firmness so dark and malignant upon it that she dared not disobey him. Slowly she descended the steep ladder into the gloomy cabin, and she felt as though she were going in fact to the damp and awful tomb. It was no high, clean and tidy cabin which may be found on board our trim packets; but it was dirty, the furniture was broken and disorderly, and a vile odor haunted the place — the combined effluvia of bilge water, greasy cooking, and mouldy woollens.

She seated herself on a locker before one of the bunks, which, in place of a berth-sack, was furnished with old coats and ragged garments covered with slush and dirt. To a young lady brought up amid the refinements of wealth and taste, it was a loathsome hole, and Bessie sighed for the pure, fresh air of the open deck. By this time the men had removed the stops from the mainsail, and the sail was hoisted. The canvas was thus removed from a skylight in the deck, and the sun shed his bright rays down into the gloomy cabin, removing some of its sombre aspect, but revealing more clearly the filth and disorder of the place.

Then the poor girl, sick at heart, and made nearly so at a less poetical organ by the vile odors of her floating tomb, heard the rattling of the chain cable as the anchor was hoisted. She looked up the companionway, and saw the jib fly up on its stay, and the vessel swing round to her course. The rudder creaked, the schooner heeled over, and she heard the waves rippling under the counter. The Griffin was in motion, and a few minutes would decide whether Dock Vincent intended to put her · on board The Starry Flag or not. It was a moment of terrible anxiety to her.

She could not think of any possible reason why Dock Vincent should wish to keep her on board of his vessel. She could not see what he was to gain by it. But, pure, innocent maiden, she had no suspicion of the wickedness which lurks in some men's hearts. She had read, but never realized, that some will sell their souls for the gold which perishes in the using. She could not believe that Dock meant any harm to her, or even that he meant to detain her on board beyond a few hours.

The Griffin rose and fell on the long billows, as she sped on her way, whither Bessie knew not, though she still hoped that she should be delivered over to the charge of the gallant Levi, in whom she had almost as much confidence as in her own father; for his mild eye, his gentle bearing, and his noble conduct, invited her admiration, and assured her she might trust him.

The moments were long and heavy to her. She glanced at her watch, and found that it was five o'clock. She could not tell which way the vessel was sailing, nor where she was. Dock did not come near her again, though she occasionally heard his voice over her head, as he stood at the helm and gave his orders to the men on the forecastle. She wanted to go on deck, but she dared not do so, for she feared the act would bring the frowns and the abuse of the evil man upon her.

The main cabin of the Griffin had four berths, only two of which appeared to be used by the men, the other two being occupied as places for storage. Bessie had already discovered two doors at the after part of the cabin. She ventured to open one of these, and found a diminutive state-room, in which was one of the stern windows of the vessel. Eagerly she looked out upon the heaving sea, to obtain some intelligence which would indicate the fate in store for her; and hope almost deserted her sinking heart when she found that the Griffin was headed from the land, at least two miles off. She could see the high wall or breakwater which protected Old Pier.

Off in another direction she could see Straitsmouth Light, which Levi had pointed out to her when she was sailing with him on Saturday afternoon. She knew that The Starry Flag, in going to Thatcher's Island, the destination of the pleasure party, must pass very near to this light-house. It was absolutely certain, therefore, that Dock Vincent did not mean to keep his promise.

She threw herself on a bench in the little state-room, which was hardly high enough to permit her to stand up, and wept as though her heart would break. The tears which had refused to flow before came freely now. Then she knelt down and said all the prayers she had ever learned from her mother's lips. They afforded her some comfort; but the future was so big and black with terrors that no peace came even from prayer, though her heart was strengthened by her devotions.

While she was still gazing at the distant land, she heard the step of Dock Vincent on the cabin ladder. Fearing that he would abuse her for presuming to enter the state-room, she hastily returned to the cabin, closing the door behind her.

"O, Mr. Dock!" cried she, as he stepped down upon the cabin floor.

"Well, what's the matter now?" demanded he, with brutal coarseness.

"Will you tell me what you are going to do with me?" pleaded the poor girl.

"If it makes any difference to you, I will. I'm going to make some money out of you."

"If you will put me on shore again, my father will give you all the money you want," sobbed Bessie.

"I know he will, but not yet," sneered Dock.

"Do put me on shore; I will give you my watch if you will."

"Let me see it."

She gave him the watch and chain.

"I'll see about it," he replied, putting the watch into his pocket.

The "little plan" appeared thus far to be a success.

CHAPTER XVIII.

THE STARRY FLAG GOES TO SEA.

ISN'T she a nice boat!" exclaimed Jenny Robarts, as The Starry Flag bounded over the long waves that rolled in from the open sea.

"Perfectly splendid!" replied Estelle.

"She is a good sea boat — isn't she, Levi?" asked the more practical Charley Manning.

"She is the best sea boat on the Cape. After what she went through in the squall off Brace's Cove, the other day, I am satisfied that she will stand anything," replied Levi, with enthusiasm. "I shouldn't be afraid to cross the Atlantic in this boat."

"Cross the Atlantic!" ejaculated John Marshall.

"I mean so," added Levi, quietly. "She behaves like a lady in a heavy sea. She don't stick her nose into it, like a pig; but she jumps over the waves, and don't make any fuss about it either. I don't

18

suppose she would be very comfortable to cross the ocean in; but so far as the safety is concerned, I would just as lief do it as not."

"I shouldn't want to go with you," said Jenny.

"I shouldn't want to have you," replied Levi, rather ungallantly. "I don't like to have girls round when it blows hard."

"You would like to have Bessie Watson round whether it blows or not," pouted Jenny.

"I don't think I should," continued Levi. "When girls get wet and drabbled, they feel mean, and want to go ashore."

"Bessie wouldn't, if you were in the boat, Levi," interposed Estelle. "She thinks you are the great-est man in the world — except her father."

"Bessie is a nice little girl, and she didn't make any fuss about it even when she got carried off by the sea the other day; but I don't believe in any girls going on the water in rough weather; it isn't the place for them. Women can't vote, and they ought to stay at home when it blows hard; besides, they are all the time getting seasick."

"Pooh! men get seasick too," replied Jenny, smartly.

Levi knew that some men did get seasick; but he had not much respect for such men, and he permitted the argument to go against him, for he had come to some rather difficult navigation needing attention at the entrance to Boat Cove. The young fisherman was good for any problem in sailing a boat, and the Flag was run safely through the cove to the two piers, which yawned, like the half-closed jaws of some gigantic monster, at the entrance to the dock.

"She isn't here!" shouted Charley Parsons, from the end of Central Wharf, as the boat approached.

"Where is she?" demanded Levi.

"A man says he told her you were at Old Pier, and she has gone over there to find you."

"Run over and tell her we are here, Charley," said Levi, vexed at the delay.

Charley Parsons hastened away to execute his commission, while Levi ran The Starry Flag into the dock, and moored her at the steps on Central Wharf. In fifteen minutes the messenger returned, having been unable to find Bessie.

"I don't understand it," said Levi, who would as

soon have thought of going to Thatcher's Island without the boat as without Bessie.

"Nor I either," replied Charley. "She wasn't on the pier, or anywhere round there."

It was decided that the whole party should land and go in search of Bessie. In half an hour one of them reported that he had met a boy who had seen Bessie going out towards Mike's Point.

"It's after five o'clock now, and it's no use to think of going down to Thatcher's Island to-night," said Levi, quite as much disappointed as any of his party when he had reached this prudent conclusion. "We must put it off till to-morrow afternoon; but if you like, I will take you round to Mike's Point, and see if we can find Bessie."

Of course live boys and girls could not decline this invitation, and The Starry Flag cast off from the steps, and ran out of the dock. When she had passed the breakwater, Levi saw the Griffin, standing off to the north-east; and though he wondered where she was going in that direction, he did not suspect that Bessie Watson was an involuntary passenger on board of her. Levi ran the boat in as near to

Knowlton's Beach as the depth of water would permit, then rounded Mike's Point, and skirted Back Beach till he came to Old Pier, having obtained a full view of the shore for half a mile, without discovering Bessie.

"I can't think where she is," said Levi; and he made fast the painter to the pier. "We must give up the trip for to-day; but if you will all be here at four o'clock to-morrow, we will go then."

With blank faces the disappointed party reluctantly landed, for it was only a partial compensation to know that the excursion would take place the next day. Levi, after locking up the cuddy, in which the materials for the feast had been placed, landed himself; for, though it was of no consequence, now that the trip had been postponed, where Bessie was, he was curious to know what had become of her. Attended by his party, he went up to Mr. Babson's. Mrs. Watson was very much surprised to learn that Levi had not seen her daughter, who had not been home since she left to take the excursion. Levi and his companions volunteered to continue the search for Bessie, as her mother appeared to be anxious

18 *

about her, though no one suspected that any harm had befallen her.

At seven o'clock, when Mr. Watson returned from Boston, Bessie had not been found, and anxiety had given place to alarm in the mind of her fond and devoted mother. The search was no longer left to the girls and boys, but the constables and all the available men and women were inquiring at the houses, and examining all of the out of the way places in the town. At nine o'clock the most searching investigation assured the agonized father and mother that she was not in the town. It was feared that she had fallen into the water, or over some rocky cliff, and it was believed that her lifeless form would be found, if found at all, in the water, or mangled beneath some jagged steep.

The people of the town — warm-hearted and tender to those in sorrow and suffering — were full of sympathy for Bessie's father and mother, whose cup of grief seemed to be full to the brim, and everything was done which the power of man could accomplish to find the lost one.

The meeting between Dock Vincent and Bessie had taken place on the extremity of Mike's Point, behind the rocks, where no one on the shore side could see them; and no person appeared to have noticed the maiden in the boat as her captor conveyed her to the Griffin.

At nine o'clock in the evening, after the village and its surroundings had been thoroughly searched, Levi went down to Old Pier, where his boat lay, intending to run along the shore in her, with a faint hope of obtaining some tidings of the lost one.

"Gracious!" exclaimed Levi, as he stepped upon the half deck of the Flag.

This ejaculation was called forth by the thought which suddenly flashed upon him that he had seen the Griffin go to sea about the time Bessie so strangely disappeared. Levi sat down in the standing room to gather up his ideas.

"That's so!" said he, bringing his fist down with tremendous energy upon the half deck. "I'll bet my life this is some of Dock Vincent's doings! What did he mean by the little plan he wanted me to help him about? That's what's the matter!"

Suddenly the young skipper jumped up as though he had been harpooned, cast loose his sails, hoisted them, and shoved off from the pier. The wind was still west, and blowing a six-knot breeze. Running out of the dock, he headed The Starry Flag to the north-east, — the direction in which the Griffin had departed, — and seated himself at the helm for a further consideration of the circumstances of the extraordinary occasion. He recalled all that he could remember of what Dock had said about his "little plan." He had been satisfied from the beginning that the unprincipled skipper of the Griffin intended to extort a large sum of money from the father of Bessie; but he had never suspected that he meant to do so by resorting to such a desperate scheme as the abduction of the little maiden.

"I'll follow him to the end of the earth; and I'll find him too!" said Levi, out loud, as The Starry Flag dashed along on her course through the gloom of the night. "I wish I had spent some of my money in buying a revolver, for I shall want it now; and I'd shoot him, after this, just as quick as I would a

dead cat! I wonder where he's gone to. That's
what I'd like to know just now. If Dock isn't a
fool, then the fools are all dead. He'll get his neck
stretched, or spend some of his life in a cage for
this job."

There were a compass and a lantern on board of
The Starry Flag, the former having been left in her
by Mr. Hatch, to be used in case of fog, while the
latter had been procured that day by Levi, to enable
him to read in the cuddy after dark. He was so
familiar with the coast that he did not need the
compass at present; but he placed it on the seat
under the tiller, and lighted the lantern to enable
him to see its face.

But where had Dock Vincent gone with his fair
prisoner? This was the all-important question to
Levi. It was impossible to answer it. The villain
had been stupid enough to mention that he had a
"little plan," but he had not been fool enough to tell
what it was. The Griffin had gone to the north-east
— that was all the adventurous young skipper had
to guide him, and for several hours he stood on in
that direction.

Levi was not proficient in the science of navigation, but he had some valuable information on the subject, entirely practical in its character. He made the proper allowance for the variation of the compass, which he had learned from the skipper of a fisherman. The Griffin was an old stunt-bowed craft, that could not make more than four knots in a seven-knot breeze, and Levi was confident that the Flag, small as she was comparatively, would outsail her. If he could only get on the right course, he was pretty sure that he could overtake her.

When well off the land, the skipper of the Flag supped on cold ham, cakes, and lemonade. He was satisfied that he had undertaken a big job; but he was determined to put it through. The Griffin had four hours the start of him, but the sail-boat was new and clean, and the chances were in her favor.

About two hours out from land, The Starry Flag ran close to a large schooner laden with lumber. Levi hailed her, and was informed by the man at the helm that she had passed close to an old vessel with a great square patch in her foresail, just at dusk.

"That's the Griffin!" exclaimed the delighted skipper of the Flag, as he filled away again; and all night long he stood on his course to the north-east.

The next morning, not only Bessie Watson, but Levi and The Starry Flag were missing.

CHAPTER XIX.

DOCK VINCENT'S LETTER.

BESSIE'S watch was a beautiful little gold one, given to her by her father. Though she valued it very highly both as a gift and for its own sake, she hardly thought of her loss when Dock Vincent very coolly put the watch and chain into his pocket. It was worth as much as The Starry Flag had cost, but no earthly goods seemed to have any value at all to her then. Her terrible situation was all she could think of, and she feared she should never again see her father and mother.

The evil man was a constant terror to her. She was afraid of him; and his ugly eye looked to her like the eye of a demon. She was love, and purity, and truth; he was all that is gross, and vile, and wicked.

"You will put me on shore, Mr. Dock — won't

you? I will not ask you for my watch if you will," said Bessie.

"You needn't be at all alarmed, Miss Bessie; I won't hurt a hair of your head, nor let any one else do so. You are just as safe here as you would be in your father's house, though I suppose it isn't quite so comfortable a place," replied Dock, who might have felt some remorse at the grief and pain he had caused in the heart of the poor girl.

"What have you done this for, Mr. Dock? Why are you sailing away with me from my parents? Won't you please to inform me? Perhaps, if you will tell me what you want, I can help you to get it."

"Perhaps you can," replied Dock, musing; "but we won't talk about that to-night."

"Won't you tell me where you are going?" pleaded Bessie.

"I hardly know myself; but don't go to being frightened, for, I tell you again, no one shall hurt you. There is one of those little state-rooms that you can have all to yourself. You may go in there, and lock yourself in. But you haven't had any supper."

19

"O, I don't want any supper. If you will only tell me, Mr. Dock, what you mean to do with me, that is all I will ask."

"I guess we won't talk about that to-night. I'll send a man down to get some supper for you, and we will talk over all these things to-morrow."

Bessie could not induce the evil man to disclose his plans to her, and she gave up the point in despair. But his solemn assurance that she should not be harmed was some comfort to her, though she felt that she could not trust him. In his rude manner he had attempted to be kind to her. He was not a pirate, nor a freebooter, for his language was as respectful as his natural coarseness would allow him to use. She sat down in the gloom of the dirty cabin, to think of the grief and anxiety which awaited her parents when her absence should be discovered. She thought her mother might suppose she had gone to Thatcher's Island in The Starry Flag, and she might not be missed till a late hour in the evening. She concluded that Levi had made the excursion without her, for he would not wish to disappoint the rest of the party.

She wept when she thought of her mother — the fond and devoted one who seemed to live only for her. She would think that her daughter was drowned, for no one could possibly suspect that she had been carried off by the evil man — by him who had saved her father's life.

Poor Bessie was as sad and miserable as she could be, and the long, gloomy night before her looked like an age of sorrow and trial.

Dock Vincent went on deck, and presently one of the two men who formed the crew of the Griffin came down into the cabin, and made a fire in the little galley, or cooking stove, which was fastened to the floor in one corner of the dingy den.

"Can you tell me where we are going?" asked Bessie of this man.

"I can't, miss; I don't know anything about it," replied the sailor. "I wash my hands of this business."

"Don't you know what Mr. Dock is going to do with me?"

"I have no idee, miss; but he says he ain't going to hurt you. You see, we sailors have to mind the cap'n, and we don't know nothin about his business; but I'll say this to you, miss: he shan't do you no hurt. Barnes and me is agreed on this point."

"My father and mother will be terribly alarmed when I don't come home," sighed Bessie.

"I shouldn't wonder if they was; but I don't see as we can do anything about it. We'll see that you ain't hurt, and if you'll keep still, we'll find out what can be done for you."

"Thank you," sobbed Bessie.

"Don't cry, miss; may be we shall be able to do something for you before morning."

"O, if you will!"

"We'll keep a lookout and see. Now, miss, what can you eat for your supper? We haven't got much, but I'll do the best I can for you. I'll brile a mackerel for you, or give you some tea and toast."

"I don't wish for anything," replied Bessie.

But Dove, the man who did the cooking, spoke so kindly to her, and pressed her so hard, that she finally consented to take some tea and toast, which he prepared for her. With much difficulty, and rather to please Dove than herself, she partook, though very sparingly, of the food, and then went to her state-room, locking the door behind her.

Dock and his men took their suppers by turns; but nothing was said about Bessie. When they went on deck, Dove and Barnes made an emphatic protest against the high crime which Dock Vincent was committing, and in which they had been compelled to take a part.

"Dove, you never saw a thousand dollars in all your life," said the unprincipled skipper; "nor you neither, Barnes. I don't ask either of you to do or say anything; but I will give you a thousand dollars apiece to keep your places in the vessel for three or four days more, or, may be, a week. Yes; and I will give you the vessel besides."

The men were tempted by this magnificent offer, as they regarded it. Dock then assured them that Bessie should be treated like a lady, and not a hair of her head harmed, and that she should be restored to her parents within three or four days. They agreed to let him know their decision in the morning; and

19 *

Dock went down into the cabin again. Taking the lantern down from the beam on which it hung, he placed it upon the table. Procuring a bottle of ink, a pen, and some paper from his state-room, he wrote for about two hours; and then, after going on deck, he turned in.

Perhaps Bessie slept a little — she could not tell, in the morning, whether she had or not; but it was the most unhappy night she had ever known. Twenty times, at least, she had prayed for herself and for her parents — that she might be saved from harm, and that they might be comforted. Dove gave her a broiled mackerel and some black coffee for her breakfast, of which she partook to please him, he had taken so much pains to suit her.

In the forenoon Dock came into the cabin, sat down at the table, and read what he had written the night before. He was still busy with the details of the "little plan." When he had read the sheet before him, he glanced at the door of Bessie's state-room, which was still closed. Then he called her name, and she came out.

"Do you want me?" asked she. "I hope you

are ready to tell me what you are going to do
with me."

"I am ready. Your father is a very rich man, I
suppose," replied Dock.

"I suppose he is," added Bessie.

"He is worth two or three hundred thousand dollars, most likely."

"I'm sure I don't know."

"Well, I know he is," continued Dock. "For a
man worth as much money, he is the meanest man
I know of."

"My father!" exclaimed Bessie, surprised and indignant.

"He gave me a hundred-dollar bill for saving
his life. That was mean."

"I am sure he will give you more if you are
not satisfied. My father gives away ever so much
money every year."

"He doesn't give it judiciously, then," said Dock,
with a sneer. "He ought to have given me at least
ten thousand dollars after I pulled him out of the
water. What good would his money have done him
if I hadn't saved his life."

."My father did not think he was in any danger himself; he told me so that day in the train."

"That's neither here nor there. He didn't pony up like a man, and I'm going to bleed him now. I suppose he won't think twenty thousand dollars is a big price to pay for you."

"For me! I don't know what you mean," answered the bewildered Bessie.

"Read this letter, then," said Dock, throwing the sheet to her.

Bessie did read it. It was a letter to her father, filled with bad spelling, and horrible grammar. It informed Mr. Watson that his daughter was on board of the Griffin, off the coast of Maine, and could only be returned to her parents when he had paid the writer twenty thousand dollars for himself, and two thousand for his men. Dock went on to say that he did not intend to fall into any trap set to catch him. If he was arrested, his men would sink the vessel, with Bessie in the cabin, in the deepest water they could find. The villain then detailed the method by which the money could be paid over to him, without imperilling the life of his daughter. Mr. Watson was directed to enclose the amount demanded in an envelope, addressed to "Captain Waldock Vincent, Bangor, Me.," and put it in the post-office. If the package reached the writer on Friday, Bessie should be sent to the principal hotel in Bangor on Saturday. The letter concluded with this ominous threat: "If you attempt to play foul, or to have me arrested, you will never see your daughter again in this world."

"But would you sink me in the vessel, Mr. Dock?" asked Bessie.

"Certainly, I would. If your father don't care enough about you to give what I ask, you ain't of much consequence; that's all."

"My father will give you the money, I know he will," said Bessie, trembling with terror at the awful threat of the evil man.

"I should say that he would; but to help the thing along, I want you to write a few lines at the end of the letter. You can advise him to take up with my offer, send the money, and not mention the matter to any constables."

"I will, Mr. Dock."

"You don't think I've treated you bad since you came aboard — do you?"

"No, Mr. Dock."

"It wouldn't do any harm to say as much; it might make your father feel better about it."

Bessie wrote half a page at the end of Dock's letter, appealing to her father to accept the offer. She added that Dock, except carrying her off, had treated her very well. The letter was sealed and directed to Mr. Watson, at Rockport.

About the middle of the afternoon, the Griffin, having been favored with a fresh and steady breeze, put into the harbor of Rockland, in Maine. Dock went ashore, and put his letter in the post office. On his return, the vessel filled away again, and after running across Penobscot Bay, came to anchor in a lonely inlet at Deer Isle. The anchor had hardly hooked into the rocks at the bottom of the little bay, before Dock's attention was attracted by a sail headed towards him.

"It seems to me I've seen that boat before," said the evil man, as the sail approached.

"I reckon you have. As sure as you live it's The Starry Flag!" replied Barnes.

CHAPTER XX.

THE CRUISE OF THE STARRY FLAG.

PERHAPS sober, staid, steady skippers, and especially prudent, plodding, non-seafaring persons, would have believed that Levi Fairfield was crazy when he sailed out in the night and the darkness into the solemn solitudes of the great ocean, cutting loose from the land, as though the salt water was his native element. It must be acknowledged that it was a bold and even reckless venture; but it was not a hopeless one; it was not one in which a skilful and daring fellow might not reasonably expect, if not a perfect success, at least enough to justify the hazard under such desperate circumstances as those under which the young fisherman commenced his voyage.

Levi did a great deal of thinking and reasoning, balanced a great many probabilities, and finally reached a conclusion which satisfied himself, and gave him the nerve and the courage to persevere to the end in his purpose. After all that Dock Vincent had darkly hinted about his "little plan," the marine philosopher at the helm of The Starry Flag was assured that he had abducted Bessie Watson, intending to extort a large sum of money from the father for her safe return. This was the first point settled.

Levi knew that Dock Vincent had formerly been the captain of a coaster plying between ports on the Penobscot and the cities of Boston and New York. The Griffin had gone off headed to the north-east, and the information he had obtained from the helmsman of the lumber vessel indicated that she was still sailing in that direction. Dock would not be likely to make a port near the Cape, to which the excitement attending the absence of Bessie might extend. It was more probable that he would proceed to some more distant harbor. His knowledge of the coast at the mouth of the Penobscot would induce him to go there. This was the second point settled.

The Griffin was an "old tub," and though she was a vessel of sixty tons, Levi was confident that The Starry Flag would outsail her in an ordinary sea, with anything less than a gale of wind blowing. Though she was a new boat, she had already made a reputation as a fast sailer, having actually run fifteen miles in an hour and ten minutes, which is very remarkable sailing for a boat of her size, and of course it was accomplished under the most favorable circumstances. Levi, therefore, did not make his calculations without knowing what he was about.

The Griffin had four hours the start of him, but she could not be, as the wind had blown, more than twenty miles ahead of him. The Flag was making seven knots, while the Griffin could not be making more than four or five. Levi expected to see the old schooner in the morning, and to be well up with her by the time she made the coast of Maine; but even if he did not see her, he was determined to continue on his course, for he could land at some place, and obtain the "ship news" to guide him.

Before daybreak the skipper of The Starry Flag could not help thinking how comfortable it would be if he could turn in and sleep a few hours, for he gaped fearfully, and his eyes were heavy; but he took a lunch, drank some lemonade, and walked briskly up and down the standing room a few times, which had the effect to wake him up. The boat went along at a lively pace over the great billows, as dry and comfortable as a lady's parlor. A little spray broke on the half deck at times, but not a drop soiled the Sunday clothes of Levi; for he had dressed himself in his best in honor of the party he was to convey to Thatcher's Island. The wind was abaft the beam, and the sails hardly needed any attention. He had only to watch the compass, and keep the boat headed north-east by north, which he had heard was the proper point for a vessel bound to Penobscot Bay.

At daylight, The Starry Flag seemed to be alone on the vast ocean. She was out of sight of land, and no other sail was to be seen. Levi was wide awake now, and it was no longer difficult for him to keep his eyes open. It was grand, sublime, the waste of waters around him rolling and beating like the pulse of the Infinite. Levi's was not a rude, coarse nature, upon which a prospect so sublime could produce no impression. He was moved, awed by it, and by the fact that he was at least fifty miles from the shore. He thought of Him who spread out this desert of waters, and his matin prayer was more real and earnest than ever before. The mission in which he was engaged was in harmony with these lofty reflections, and no childish fear moved him to look back from the purpose to which he had nobly devoted himself.

The sun rose bright and beautiful from his ocean bed, and Levi was almost inspired by the grandeur of the scene, rendered ten times more sublime by the circumstances of his situation. As the bright, warm rays of the sun poured down upon him at a later hour, the wind hauled a little more to the northward, and freshened considerably, but not so that the Flag could not carry her jib and mainsail. Levi was disappointed, but not discouraged, because nothing was to be seen of the Griffin. The captain, crew, and all hands, piped to breakfast, when the sun had dried the decks of the boat. The lockers were still plentifully supplied with cold ham, bread, cheese, and cake, and the meal was sumptuous.

While Levi was thus engaged, he caught sight of a distant sail — so distant that he could hardly make it out. It was off on his weather beam, hull down, with only the upper part of her sails in sight. The young skipper watched her with deep interest; and when he had finished his breakfast, he took from the cuddy a spy-glass, which he had borrowed of Mr. Gayles, to enable Bessie to look at distant objects, during the trip to Thatcher's Island, and carefully examined the stranger. But she was too far off for him to make her out. By this time two schooners were in sight to leeward of him, but both of them were bound to the southward.

As Levi watched the distant sail till it became evident to him that she was going to the northward, he altered his course so as to approach near enough to her in a short time to make her out. He was tolerably confident, after he had studied the situation, that this vessel was the Griffin, and he began

20 *

to be somewhat excited at the prospect. An hour later, he discerned through the spy-glass the great square patch on the foresail, and his belief was fully confirmed. Dock had kept a point nearer to the westward than Levi, who in a few hours more would have passed the Griffin, and left her behind him.

Levi decided that it would not be prudent for him to exhibit The Starry Flag to Dock Vincent; so he just barely kept the Griffin's sails in sight, keeping abreast, and a little ahead of her, till he sighted the land in the middle of the afternoon. The young fisherman was now worked up to a tremendous pitch of enthusiasm. He was so excited that he forgot all about his dinner till his abused stomach clamored for attention. For three hours the islands of Penobscot Bay surrounded him, and Levi was compelled to get nearer to the chase.

The Griffin ran into Rockland harbor, lying to while Dock and Barnes went ashore in the boat. Levi had prudently kept at a distance, intending to wait till the vessel anchored, and then to board her after dark, with the assistance of some officers to be obtained in the town. He ran into the bay

as far as Jameson's Point; but, as we have narrated
in the last chapter, the Griffin remained only a short
time in the harbor. When Levi saw her coming
down the bay, he stood off and sheltered his boat
from the observation of those on board the schooner
by running her behind Owl's Head until she had
passed, when he followed her again, at a safe
distance.

As the chase was now headed to the north-east,
Levi was sure that she intended to make another
harbor. It was nearly sundown when she came to
anchor in the lonely bay at Deer Isle. As the Griffin swung round at her moorings, Levi surveyed the
harbor which Dock had chosen. There was not a
house in sight, and the pursuer knew nothing whatever of the geography of the place. As he saw none,
he concluded there were no inhabitants near the
place, and that the skipper of the Griffin had chosen
his anchorage with reference to this fact.

Levi did not know the name of the town at which
Dock had landed; he could only see that it was a
large place. But he rightly conjectured that the
conspirator had gone ashore there to make his

demand upon Mr. Watson through the post-office.

The bold young skipper was troubled by the situation, and was at a loss what to do. He could not hope to obtain any help from the shore, and he was hardly able to do battle with the three men on the deck of the Griffin. He could not anchor outside of the bay, the water was so deep, and he was afraid the Griffin might change her position in the night if he remained out of sight of her. As he reflected, and felt that the chances were now against him, he became desperate, and under this impulse he stood boldly into the lonely bay, direct for the chase.

Without showing his face, or answering the hail of Dock Vincent, he ran The Starry Flag alongside the schooner, and made fast her painter to the fore shrouds. With the short, heavily-ironed boat-hook of the little craft in his hand, he leaped upon the deck of the Griffin.

"Is that you, Levi?" demanded Dock, almost paralyzed by the appearance of the youth at this inopportune time.

"I'll bet it's me!" answered Levi, nearly choked by his deep emotion.

"How came you here, Levi?" continued Dock, who seemed disposed to adopt a conciliatory course.

"I came after Bessie Watson, and I'm going to have her too," said Levi, decidedly.

"Bessie Watson? She isn't here."

"O, Mr. Dock! Do let me go with him," interposed Bessie, whose head appeared at the companion-way, as she climbed the steep steps.

"That lie's nailed!" said Levi, moving towards the villain.

"Go below again!" added Dock, sternly.

"Don't mind him, Bessie," replied Levi.

"What are you going to do about it, Levi Fairfield?" demanded Dock, roused to anger by the conduct of the young fisherman. "Here, Dove, you and Barnes pitch this fellow into his boat, and I will take care of the girl."

"I washed my hands of this business in the beginning, and I won't have anything to do with it," replied Dove.

"Nor I neither," added Barnes.

"Cowards!" sneered Dock, as he rushed towards Levi.

At this moment Bessie sprang to the deck, and her movement attracted the attention of Dock, who, fearful that his prize would escape, turned with the intention of driving her back into the cabin.

"Let her alone!" shouted Levi, angrily, as he followed Dock up to the companion-way, and seized him by the arm to prevent him from pushing Bessie down the ladder.

Dock turned upon him again, and attempted to lay his heavy hand upon him; but Levi suddenly raised the iron-shod end of the boat-hook, and brought it down with such force upon the head of the evil man that he sank senseless upon the deck.

CHAPTER XXI.

THE STARRY FLAG COMES TO ANCHOR.

"WHAT have you done, Levi?" exclaimed Bessie, as, filled with fear and horror, she saw the form of Dock Vincent drop heavily upon the deck of the Griffin.

"I don't know. I've done my duty, I hope," replied Levi, puffing under the excitement and the exertion of the moment. "I hope I haven't killed him, but I can't help it if I have."

"O, I hope not!" added Bessie.

By this time Barnes and Dove, the two seamen of the Griffin, had come aft, and they commenced an examination into the condition of Dock.

"You hit him a hard knock, Levi," said Dove, "but he isn't dead. He's only stunded, and he'll come out of it pretty soon."

"Then I'll be going, for I don't want to have any

more trouble with him. Come, Bessie, get your things, and come with me."

"He won't die — will he?" asked she, glancing, with a shudder, at the stout frame of Dock, extended on the deck.

"Bless you, Miss Bessie, he will be as well as ever in an hour or two," answered Dove. "You needn't consarn yourself about him."

"I'm very glad it's no worse."

"Come, Bessie; have you anything with you?"

"Nothing but my shawl;" and she went down into the cabin for it.

"Where you goin, Levi?" asked Dove.

"If I don't tell you, you won't know," replied the young skipper, prudently.

"See here, Levi; you don't think Barnes and me had anything to do with this thing — do you?"

"Well, I don't know that you did; but I think, if it had been my case, the old Griffin would have found her way back to Rockport before this time."

"You don't understand it, Levi," added Barnes, with an anxious look. "Captain Dock Vincent always has his own way, you know."

"So he does, when he can; but he didn't have it just now," answered Levi, looking down at the insensible form. "Why don't you take care of him, and do something for him?"

"We are goin to; but I want to know whether you think Dove and me was mixed up in this business."

"I don't know anything about it; but I think you might have prevented it, if you had been a mind to."

"'Tain't so; and we don't want you to go to blamin us for what we didn't have nothin to do with. We're hands aboard this vessel, and we have to do just what the cap'n tells us to do. You know that just as well as I do."

"I haven't anything to say about it. I don't believe you would have done such a mean thing yourself, either one of you," added Levi, evasively.

"But you ain't a goin to tell the folks down to Rockport that we helped Cap'n Dock do this thing — be you?" continued Barnes, beginning to be a little excited at the prospective loss of reputation which such a report would involve.

21

"I'll tell them just what you say — that you hadn't anything to do with the affair, and that you only obeyed your captain."

"Well, I'm satisfied with that," said Dove, as Levi handed Bessie in to The Starry Flag. "We told Cap'n Dock we wouldn't have anything to do with carryin the gal off."

"Yes, he really did; and Mr. Dove was very kind to me, and told me that he and the other man wouldn't let Mr. Dock hurt me," interposed Bessie, who was disposed to put a very charitable construction upon the action, and upon the inaction, of the two seamen, for she did not know that they had consented to receive a thousand dollars apiece for standing by the vessel till the "little plan" was fully executed.

Levi, fearful that the two men, in self-defence, might attempt to prevent his departure, did not express his mind as fully as he would have done under different circumstances. He followed Bessie into the boat, and hoisted the mainsail.

"I say, Levi, you don't think of taking the girl back to Rockport in that boat — do you?" asked Barnes.

"I should feel safer in her than I should in your old Griffin," replied the young skipper.

"It's rather resky to go off a hundred and fifty miles in an open boat like that," added the seaman.

"I don't think so," answered Levi, as he shoved off. "Why don't you go and see to your captain now?"

"Dove is lookin out for him. Well, good by, Levi; but don't be hard on us when you get back to Rockport."

"I'll tell the folks just what you say, and they may judge for themselves. Good by;" and The Starry Flag began to gather headway, and bear them away from the schooner.

Levi ran up the jib, trimmed the sails, and seated himself at the helm.

"O, I'm so happy, Levi!" exclaimed Bessie, as the Flag dashed out of the lonely bay. "You can't tell how much I have suffered since I went on that vessel!"

"I know you must have had a very bad time."

"And you have followed me all the way from Rockport?"

"Yes; I sailed all last night and all to-day, following the Griffin. I thought Dock would run into some place where there were people, and I intended to get some help, and get you away from him."

"I owe you ever so much, Levi, for what you have done! And I'm sure I don't know what would have happened if you hadn't come as you did. Did my father send you?"

"He does not even know where I am; for after I got the idea into my head that Dock was carrying you off, I didn't dare to go back to Rockport, for fear I shouldn't overtake the Griffin."

Levi told Bessie everything that had happened from the time he went to Old Pier to take his party on board up to the moment when he had boarded the Griffin with the boat-hook in his hand. The poor girl wept bitterly when she thought what her father and mother had suffered, and were still suffering, on account of her unexplained absence. When Levi assured her they would soon be in Rockport, she dried her eyes, and told her brave companion the history of her abduction, and of her stay on board the Griffin. By the time these interesting

stories were finished it was quite dark, and Levi
proposed that they should have some supper. He
lighted his lantern, and placed cold ham, bread,
crackers, and cake on the seat, with lemonade instead of tea. Under the hopeful promises of the
future, Bessie regained her appetite, and ate heartily,
much to the satisfaction of the skipper, who fully
sustained his own reputation as "a good feeder" on
the present occasion.

"Bessie, I don't know that you will like to go so
far in an open boat. I suppose it is nearly a hundred and fifty miles across to Rockport, right over
the open sea, and out of sight of land," said Levi,
after he had cleared away the remains of the supper,
and put the boat in order for her night voyage.

"There is no other way to go — is there?" asked
Bessie, rather appalled at the prospect of such a
cruise.

"Why, yes; I can put you on shore, and you
can go by the railroad or the steamboat to Boston.
There is a big town up here somewhere. The
Griffin put in there, on her way up. I haven't got
any map or chart, and I'm sure I don't know where

21 *

we are; only that we are on the coast of Maine,
and somewhere near the mouth of the Penobscot
River. All I know is, that I must stand about
south-west to bring me back to Rockport. When I
get a sight of the land over on the other side, I
shall know where we are."

"But are you not afraid to go right out to sea in
an open boat?" asked Bessie.

"Not a bit of it. I shall feel just as safe as I
should on shore," replied Levi.

"Well, if you are not afraid, I'm not, Levi," said
she, with emphasis. "You say we are somewhere
near the mouth of the Penobscot River. I have
been to Rockland and Thomaston with father.
When we returned home, we went to Portland in a
steamboat, and then to Boston by railroad."

"I suppose we are too late for any steamers to-
night, for I know those that go to Boston pass the
Cape about two or three o'clock in the morning."

"But we don't know when anything starts," added
Bessie.

"I don't know that I could find the town where
we put in this afternoon, but I think I could. If I

landed you there to-night, I don't see how you could get to Boston before to-morrow night." ·

"But the train from Portland would leave us at Beverly, and we would take the cars there for Rockport."

"Perhaps the train you would go on would not connect with one for Rockport."

"Dear me! I'm sure I don't know what to do."

"If the wind holds good, I expect to be in Rockport to-morrow afternoon; for you know I must be there on Thursday at the trial."

"I thought you would go with me by the steamboat or the railroad," said Bessie.

"I couldn't leave my boat."

"I wouldn't go without you, Levi," added she, decidedly.

"I must take my boat home."

"Then I shall go with you."

"It may come on to blow," suggested the prudent skipper.

"But it will be as safe for me as it is for you."

"The boat is safe as long as she is well handled; and I don't think there is a bit of danger at this

season of the year. I shouldn't want to go across
there in the fall or winter, though I shouldn't be
afraid to do it then; but it wouldn't be comfortable.
It would be too cold and wet."

"I shall go with you, Levi, any way."

"I can make you up a nice little bed in the cabin
there, and you can sleep all night," added Levi,
delighted with the spirit of his fair companion.

"I think I could sleep anywhere to-night, for I
believe I hardly closed my eyes last night. But
what are *you* going to do, Levi?"

"O, I must keep awake and steer the boat."

"But you didn't sleep any last night."

"Well, I will sleep enough when I get home to
make it up. But I'm afraid the wind is going to
die out," added Levi, who had been fearing this for
the last hour, for the breeze had subsided almost to
a calm.

"What will you do then?" said Bessie, with a
long gape, which suggested that it was bedtime
for her.

"Wait till the breeze comes. Let me make up

your bed for you now, and you can lie down, for I am sure you are very sleepy."

" I am, indeed."

Levi's services, unfortunately, were no longer needed at the helm, for the wind had entirely subsided, and the mainsail hung idly from the gaff. He arranged the best bed the material at his command would permit; and Bessie lay down upon it, after she had reverently repeated her prayers, to which Levi listened in the true spirit of devotion. He drew the slide over the companion-way, and partly closed the doors, so that she would not be suffocated by the closeness of the cuddy.

The Starry Flag appeared to rest motionless on the water, for there was not a breath of air. Her skipper was annoyed and impatient. He wanted to be dashing over the waves towards Rockport, with the message of gladness to the distracted parents of his fair passenger; and it was intensely provoking to have the wind die out at such a time. Worse than this, he found that the tide was coming in, and that the Flag was drifting up the bay. This would not do; he was going ahead backwards, drifting upon an island to the northward of him. He was obliged to let go the anchor to check this retrograde tendency.

The boat had come to a dead stand; and as there was nothing better that he could do, he furled his sails, fastened the lantern to the jib-stay, stretched himself on one of the seats, and went to sleep.

CHAPTER XXII.

HOMEWARD BOUND.

IT was about eleven o'clock at night, when the wind died out and the tide turned, so that The Starry Flag could make no further progress on her voyage to Cape Ann. Undoubtedly it was best that it should be so; that the elements should so far conspire against him as to prevent him from going to sea; for Levi was not in condition to stand it another night at the helm. The delay afforded him the sleep and the rest he needed so much.

It was five o'clock in the morning when the young skipper waked. The sun had risen, and was shining brightly on the silver waters, and a gentle breeze from the westward rippled the surface of the bay. Levi sprang up with a start: his first thought was, that he was wasting precious time; that he had slept hours longer than he should have done.

Without a moment of delay he hoisted the mainsail, and was going forward to get up the anchor, when he discovered a sail moving out from behind the island under whose lee the boat was moored. A second glance revealed to him the great square patch on the foresail of the Griffin, and assured him that Dock Vincent had come to his senses, and was in pursuit of him.

The noise he made in hoisting the mainsail had awakened Bessie, and she came out of the cuddy.

"Where are we, Levi? Have we got almost to Rockport?"

"We have been at anchor all night, Bessie. There comes the Griffin, and we haven't a moment to spare," replied Levi, sharply.

"O, that's terrible!" added she, glancing at the old vessel, which was now within a few rods of the boat. "What shall we do?"

"Don't be alarmed, Bessie; I can keep out of his way," added Levi, as he unbent the cable and threw the rope overboard, for he could not spare the precious moments which would be required to weigh the anchor.

"Stop, there, Levi Fairfield!" shouted Dock Vincent, from the helm of the Griffin.

"O, Levi!" gasped Bessie, when she heard the tones of her persecutor's voice.

"Don't be frightened, Bessie," interposed the gallant young skipper, in soothing tones. "He shall not have you again."

Levi hoisted the jib quicker than the jib of The Starry Flag was ever hoisted before.

"Put the helm down, Bessie — the other way; that's right;" and the Flag began to gather headway just as Dock Vincent, who had gone out on the bowsprit of the Griffin, was attempting, with a long boat-hook, to fasten to the jib-stay of the sail-boat.

"All right, Bessie," said Levi, with a feeling of intense relief, as he belayed the jib-halliard, and ran to the helm.

The mainsail was drawing, and as the Griffin came up into the wind, the Flag passed out of the reach of the evil man. Levi gathered up his jib-sheets, trimmed his head-sail, and the boat went off on her course to the southward of the island, leaving

22

the Griffin to wear round and renew the chase. It was evident that the schooner had the breeze at an early hour in the morning, and started in pursuit of Levi; and if the young skipper had slept five minutes more, his little craft would have been captured by the villain.

"I never was so frightened in my life!" exclaimed Bessie, with a long breath. "I was sure that we were lost. But he may catch us yet."

"Not he," said Levi, confidently. "The old Griffin could no more catch us than a snail could catch a streak of lightning. You are as safe now, Bessie, as you would be in the parlor of your father's house. I can't think what made me sleep so long."

"Poor fellow! I suppose you were tired out, as I was," replied Bessie, full of sympathy for her protector and friend.

"I was tired, but I didn't mean to sleep more than a couple of hours."

"I am glad you did sleep, though I supposed, when I waked up, that we had been sailing all night."

Levi explained the situation so that his fellow-voyager could understand it. Both of them watched the Griffin all the time, for it was plain that Dock had not yet abandoned his "little plan." The men on board of her were setting a staysail to increase her speed; but Levi did not borrow any trouble on this account. As long as there was any wind at all, he was sure that he could show Dock the name on the stern of his boat all day long. If the Griffin had been even a fair sailer, it would have been otherwise, and Levi would have been compelled to resort to other expedients than his heels to avoid capture.

The Starry Flag gained on the schooner until they were about a quarter of a mile apart; and then Bessie began to feel some assurance that she would not again fall into the clutches of the evil man. The wind was very light, and neither craft was making more than four knots an hour.

"I don't like to ask you to be ship's steward, Bessie, but I think it is breakfast time, and I don't like to leave the helm even for a minute," said Levi, when he felt sure that, with careful management, he could keep out of the Griffin's way.

"O, I should like something to do!" exclaimed Bessie, springing to her feet.

"Should you? Well, then, you may bring out the breakfast. It's just the same as we had for supper, and as we shall have for dinner. You will find it in that locker," continued Levi, pointing to the place where he had deposited the ship's provisions.

"I'm sure it's good enough."

"If I had thought of having a lady passenger, I might have provided better for her."

"Why, it's as good as you have yourself, and I'm sure I don't want anything better."

Levi wished he had a cup of tea or coffee for her, and for himself too, for that matter; but there was still plenty of cold water and lemonade on board, and the cake was not half used. Bessie arranged the provision on one of the seats as tastefully and neatly as the material would permit, and the captain, crew, and passengers all breakfasted at one table, the skipper keeping his place at the helm, with an eye on the Griffin all the time.

The relative positions of the Flag and the schooner

were not materially changed during the forenoon. Four miles an hour, to one as impatient as Levi, was very slow progress, and to make this he had the advantage of the ebb tide. At noon the boat was still among the islands of Penobscot Bay, having made not more than thirty miles during the half day. The breeze did not increase, and against the tide, after it had turned, the progress was still more unsatisfactory. Several schooners were in sight, bound down the bay, which kept the young voyagers company, and helped to quiet the fears of Bessie, who relied upon these people for help in case the evil man should attempt to capture her again.

"I think this is rather tiresome, Levi," said Bessie, after they had been to dinner.

"Confounded tiresome!" replied the skipper, earnestly.

"Don't you suppose there will be more wind than this before night?"

"I can't tell; but I'm afraid not. It looks to me just as though we were going to have dull, muggy weather, with Paddy's hurricane to boot."

"A hurricane?"

22*

"Don't be scared — only Paddy's hurricane," laughed Levi.

"What's that?"

"A hurricane that blows up and down — in other words, a dead calm."

"O, I hope not."

"I hope not; but I am more afraid of a calm than I am of a blow. I must be in Rockport to-morrow forenoon, you know."

"You must, if you can," said Bessie.

"What will my uncle and the rest of them think if I am not there when the trial takes place? I must be there!" added Levi, anxiously.

"And my poor father and mother don't know where I am!" sighed Bessie.

Then both of them went to thinking, and the boat rose and fell on the billows, hardly going forward at all. But about four o'clock in the afternoon the breeze freshened up, and it blew quite briskly for two or three hours. Levi brightened up, and looked as happy as a lord. His tongue flew like a bobbin as the boat passed the last range of islands, and stood out upon the open sea. Bessie was as merry as a cricket, for the bounding little craft was swiftly bearing her to the arms of her affectionate parents.

"There comes the old Griffin," said Levi. "She is doing better than I ever saw her do before. I declare she has rigged her gaff-topsails. I didn't know she had any before."

"Will she catch us, Levi?"

"No, I think not," replied the young skipper; but he was somewhat anxious on the subject.

If the breeze should increase so as to create a heavy sea, the Griffin might be able to carry sail longer than the Flag, and thus overhaul her; but Levi hoped for the best, and paid close attention to sailing his boat. The schooner, by the aid of her gaff-topsails and staysail, kept about even with the Flag until nearly sunset, when the wind again died out, and left the boat rolling and pitching uneasily on the glassy billows.

"Here we are again," said Levi, impatiently. "We have come to a dead stand-still."

"I'm so sorry!" replied Bessie, sharing the disappointment of her companion.

"I expected to be in sight of land on the other side before this time," added Levi; "and here we are, in sight of land on this side. I am sorry I didn't land you at some place, and let you go home in the steamboat, or by the cars."

"Well, it can't be helped now, Levi, and we may as well make the best of it," replied Bessie, who felt it her duty to be cheerful under the trying circumstances.

"Of course we can't help ourselves, and we may as well laugh as cry. All we can do is to whistle for a breeze. But I'm afraid I shall not get to Rockport in season for the trial."

"Don't you be concerned about that, Levi. When my father finds out what you have done for me, he will make it all right. My father knows the governor, — he has been to our house in Boston, — and I'm sure he can help you."

"I don't like to have my uncle telling them he knew I would run away, and all that sort of thing.

But if I can only get you through all right, Bessie, I shall be satisfied, even if I do have to go to prison."

"You shall not go to prison, Levi!" answered Bessie, firmly. "If you do, I will go with you."

"That wouldn't do any good. I ought not to think of myself at all, and I won't any more. I will do the best I can, and I won't trouble my head any more about the trial, or my uncle, or the prison, or anything else."

"You are a good boy, Levi; and God will protect you, whatever happens ; but I say you shall not be sent to prison. I will go to the governor myself, and on my knees —"

"Hallo!" shouted Levi, suddenly springing to his feet.

"What is the matter, Levi?" asked Bessie, alarmed by his movements and his words.

"Dock Vincent is getting out his boat!"

"What for?"

"Why, he is going to row the jolly-boat over to us," said Levi, seizing the short boat-hook with which he had done such good service before.

The Griffin had swung round, so that Levi could see those on board lowering the jolly-boat, which was suspended at the stern davits. They saw Dock and one of his men get into the boat, and pull towards The Starry Flag.

Bessie trembled.

CHAPTER XXIII.

THE NIGHT AND THE GALE.

WHAT will become of us Levi?" exclaimed Bessie, as she saw the jolly-boat of the Griffin approaching The Starry Flag.

"Don't be frightened, Bessie. We shall get out of this scrape some how or other, just as we have done before. In my opinion we shall have a breeze soon from the southward and westward, and all, or a little more of it, than we want," replied Levi; but his words had hardly any meaning, even to himself.

"What can we do if he comes to take me? He won't let you hit him with that boat-hook again."

"He shall not take you out of this boat, Bessie, while I'm alive!" added Levi, with a suggestive shake of the head. "I wish I had a pistol or a gun."

"You wouldn't shoot him — would you, Levi?"

"Just as quick as I would shoot a gull, or smash the head of a dog-fish."

Still the jolly-boat of the Griffin continued to approach, and the defences of The Starry Flag were as unsatisfactory as before. Levi was anxious, and he could not decide what he should do. He could not hope successfully to resist so powerful a man as Dock Vincent, assisted now, it might be, by one of his men.

"He is almost here, Levi," said Bessie, in terror.

"I know he is; and all we can do is to wait for him," replied Levi, with a coolness which was wholly assumed, for he had but little confidence in his ability to defend his fair companion.

"What shall I do?" repeated she.

"Leave it all to me, Bessie; I will do the best I can. You had better go into the cuddy, and keep out of sight."

The terrified girl went into the little cabin, and seated herself on the low berth, to wait, in awful suspense, the result of Dock's intended visit.

"Better keep off!" shouted Levi, as the jolly-boat came within hail of the Flag.

Dock paid no attention to the hail, and Levi grasped the iron-shod boat-hook in the most determined manner, fully resolved to fight rather than permit his passenger to be taken from his protection; and to fight as long as the boat-hook held together, and he could keep his head above his shoulders.

"Better keep off!" shouted he again.

"I want to see you, Levi," said Dock, as he and his man stopped rowing, when the jolly-boat was within twenty feet of The Starry Flag.

"Don't come any nearer, if you know when you are well off! I won't stand no nonsense," replied the young skipper, as resolutely as though he had had his hand on the lock-string of a twenty-four pounder, with whose iron messenger he could have sent the jolly-boat and her crew to the bottom at his own pleasure.

"I want to talk with you, Levi," added Dock.

"Talk as much as you like, but don't come any nearer."

"I owe you one for the rap you gave me last night, but I will call that square, if you will do

23

the right thing now," continued Dock, as he pulled a couple of strokes with his oar.

"Stop there!" bellowed Levi, fiercely. "Don't you come any nearer. I don't want to shoot you."

"Have you got a pistol?"

"If you come any nearer you will find out whether I have or not."

It was more than probable that Dock would find out whether Levi had a pistol or not, if he lessened the distance between the two boats; but the hint had a salutary effect upon the villanous captain of the Griffin. He did not seem disposed to test the question, for wretches like him are generally cowards.

"I only want to talk with you, Levi," continued Dock.

"Talk away as much as you please. I don't care how much you talk, though I'd just as lief hear it thunder."

"I want to settle up this business."

"You can't settle it with me."

"Yes, I can. I didn't mean to hurt the girl."

"No matter what you meant," retorted Levi.

"If you'll come aboard my vessel, Levi, I'll make it all right with you. If you want to make five or six thousand dollars, I can put you in the way of doing it."

"I don't."

"You might just as well do it as not. We won't hurt the girl."

"Shut up! You needn't talk to me in that way," said Levi, indignantly.

"But just think of it — five thousand dollars don't grow on every bush, you know. We ain't a-going to steal it, you see. I can put you in the way of getting it honestly."

"I can put you in the way of spending five or six years in the State Prison; and I'll do it if you don't sheer off, and go back to your vessel."

"My father will give you five thousand dollars, Levi," interposed Bessie, who perhaps did not know Levi well enough to understand that no money could tempt him to do a mean and wicked deed.

"I say, Levi, didn't you know it was going to blow like sixty before morning?" persisted Dock,

growing desperate at his failure to move the gallant hero of The Starry Flag.

"Let it blow," replied the young skipper.

"You will get swamped in that open boat."

"Don't trouble yourself about me," answered Levi,
now really encouraged and hopeful, for he saw the
gentle ripple of a coming breeze on the water.

Dock spoke in a low tone to Barnes, who was his
companion, and the conversation continued for a moment, and then became rather stormy. It was evident that Dock wanted to board the Flag, and take
Bessie out of her, and that Barnes was opposed to
the measure. In the bottom of the boat there was
an old rusty tin dipper, with a long handle, which
Levi picked up. Breaking off the handle, he thought
it was a tolerably good imitation of the barrel of a
pistol, and he took some pains to display it to the
men in the jolly-boat, hoping that it would quicken
their ideas of prudence and discretion.

A breath of air swelled the sails of The Starry
Flag, and she began to move off on her course again.
As the distance between her and the jolly-boat in-
creased, the wrangling between Dock and Barnes

became more earnest, and even fierce, and the last words which Levi heard, as the sail-boat gathered headway, came from the latter, and related to the pistol, as he supposed it was, which he had seen in the hands of the young skipper.

"All right, Bessie," said Levi, in cheerful tones, as the Flag went off on her course.

"O, I am so glad!" ejaculated she, joining him in the standing-room.

"I think Dock persuaded Barnes to come out here on a peaceful mission. He meant to play off a trick on me, and get us aboard the Griffin."

"But he offered to give you five thousand dollars if you would help him."

"Well, I wouldn't do it if he would give me five thousand million dollars," said Levi, laughing. "But we have got a breeze now, and I don't care whether school keeps or not."

It was now almost dark. The weather had been cloudy during the latter part of the day, and the breeze that had sprung up came from the southward. To Levi there was a dirty look all round the horizon, and he realized that he should have his hands full

23 *

before morning. He did not express his fears to Bessie in full, not wishing to terrify her, hoping she would go to sleep, and not know anything about the storm when it came. But he had full confidence in the sea-going qualities of The Starry Flag, and was quite satisfied that she could, if well handled, weather any gale that ever blew. He had tested her, and believed in her.

The darkness settled down upon the ocean, and upon the little craft. Dock had returned to the Griffin, which could not now be seen from the Flag. The wind continued to freshen, and the white caps on the dark waves could be seen in the gloom of the cloudy night.

"I think you had better turn in, Bessie," said Levi.

"Turn in?"

"Go to bed, I mean."

"Don't you think we are going to have a storm?"

"It looks like rain, certainly, and it may blow pretty hard."

"Do you think there is any danger?"

"Not a bit, Bessie. If I did think so, I should

make for the nearest land. We are much safer out here than we should be in among those islands."

"How black and gloomy it looks all around — don't it?"

"It always looks so in a cloudy night on the water. Now turn in, Bessie."

She complied rather because Levi wished it than because she wanted to do so. She lay down upon the bed her friend had made for her the night before. Levi covered her with the old sail, and propped the table-board before the front part of the berth, banking it up with a part of the covering, so that she could not roll out when the boat pitched violently, as the skipper knew she would before morning. He then returned to the helm, lashed his lantern to the seat, and carefully secured the compass, in anticipation of the rough time he expected.

Levi heard no more of Bessie. He had closed the slide and the double doors of the cuddy; but there was a little blind in each of the latter, which in the fresh breeze would admit a sufficient supply of air. His fair charge was safe and comfortable, and Levi turned his whole attention to the boat. Within an hour after he had completed his preparations, it was blowing decidedly fresh; but The Starry Flag, still under all sail, was going at a fierce rate through the water, and not laboring very heavily. She was close-hauled, or nearly so, and her skipper judged that she was making about eight knots an hour — a rate which was entirely satisfactory to him.

At midnight it blew a summer gale. Levi had furled the jib, and put two reefs in his mainsail; but the Flag behaved admirably, and still held her course.

At two o'clock in the morning, by Levi's time, — which was all guess work, and might have varied two hours, — it rained in torrents; but the gale had subsided in a measure, and one reef had been turned out of the mainsail. It was "all well" on board, though Levi was drenched to the skin. As long as the boat went ahead at a good round rate, he did not care for anything else. It seemed hardly possible that Bessie could sleep through the whole of it, for the Flag in the heavy seas seemed almost to stand up straight at times; the waves broke in heavy volumes on the half deck over her head, and the air was filled with terrific howls. If she was awake, she said nothing.

At daylight, on Thursday morning, the gale had moderated into a fresh breeze, but it had hauled to the westward, so that Levi could not lay his course. He had turned out his reefs in the mainsail, and hoisted the jib. The sea had gone down considerably, and there was every prospect of a pleasant day.

At seven o'clock, judged by the height of the sun, the boat was running in towards White Island Light, on the Isles of Shoals. Bessie had turned out, and declared that she never slept better in her life, and that The Starry Flag was a "perfect love" of a boat.

The court at Rockport was to come in at ten o'clock, and Levi was still twenty miles from his destination; but he had run in shore far enough to get a slant, and was sure that he could "fetch" inside of Straitsmouth on the home tack. Bessie brought out the provisions, and "all hands" breakfasted on board, as they hoped, for the last time, on that cruise.

CHAPTER XXIV.

THE RETURN OF THE STARRY FLAG.

THE excitement which followed the disappearance of Bessie Watson had only partially subsided on Thursday forenoon, when Mr. Fairfield, Ruel Belcher, the constable, and others, assembled at the office of Squire Saunders for the continuation of the examination of Levi. It was a mere form, for the defendant was not in town, and of course the trial could not proceed. The two gentlemen who had given bail for the appearance of Levi were not in a very pleasant frame of mind, for the young man had neither been seen nor heard of since Monday night.

Without delaying the current of our story long enough to detail all the efforts which had been used to find Bessie, the search had been as thorough as wealth and energy could make it. All the towns on the coast from Boston to Portsmouth had been visited, all the shores had been examined, all the ponds dragged, and all the out-of-the-way places explored. Fishermen, sailors, and landsmen had been employed, and during Tuesday and Wednesday there was not an idle person within ten miles of Rockport, and the busiest of them all was Mr. Gayles, the constable.

The absence of Levi Fairfield was not discovered till Tuesday forenoon; and even then it was supposed that he had gone after dog-fish, as usual, in his boat; but in the evening, when he did not return, and nothing had been heard of him, it was believed that something unusual had occurred to him. Mr. Watson thought it very singular that Levi should thus absent himself at a time when Bessie's parents were in such a state of agonizing suspense.

By Wednesday noon, when Levi's absence was continued, Mr. Fairfield began to be hopeful that his ward had actually departed, never more to return. It was not consistent with his ideas to believe anything good of Levi; and by this time he had fully satisfied himself that the boy had run away

— that he feared to face the results of the examination. Some thought the young fisherman had ventured too far out to sea, and that The Starry Flag
had been swamped and sunk, carrying the bold
youth down with her; and others that he had
sold the boat in some port not yet visited, and
"left for parts unknown." Mr. Fairfield did not
care which was true, if one of them could only
be fully established.

The miser was apt to be a fast reasoner. What
he wished to believe, he generally succeeded in
making out to be true. On Wednesday afternoon,
he was pretty well satisfied that Levi would not
come back to Rockport again. With this belief
and confidence, he once more drew the two hundred and fifty dollars — the identical bills paid to
Levi by Mr. Watson — from their hiding-place, and
put them in his pocket. Cunning and avaricious men
often overreach themselves; and it would have been
better for him, though worse for the ends of truth
and justice, if he had permitted the money to remain
in its hiding-place. He went to Gloucester that
afternoon, to see a man who had applied to him

for a loan of five hundred dollars at an exorbitant rate of interest. He passed the bills, with an equal amount from his own funds, to this person, with the understanding that the money was to be expended in Boston the next day.

The desire to obtain the extra and illegal interest had tempted him to use the bills, which actually belonged to Levi, before it was prudent — as rogues use this word — to do so. But the bills would go off to Boston, and would soon be scattered, and all traces of them lost. Mr. Fairfield really believed that he was shrewd, and that it would not be possible for the bank notes to appear against him. He rubbed his hands with delight when he had finished the business, and did not even grudge the thirty cents he had expended in railroad fares — which was more extraordinary than any other part of the transaction.

Mr. Gayles had some views of his own in regard to the disappearance of Bessie Watson and the continued absence of Levi. Mr. Watson had more confidence in him than in any other person, because he had been so energetic in the search, and because, from the beginning, he had spoken words of hope to the distracted parents. When Levi's bail grumbled, Mr. Gayles declared that the boy had not run away; he was certain that he would come back. And Mr. Watson assured the grumblers, that, whether Levi came back or not, he would pay the bail if it should be forfeited.

"Mr. Watson, you don't know Levi Fairfield as well as I do," said the constable. "I have had some dealings with him, and I know him through and through. You may take my word for it, he hasn't run away; and more than that, I'll be willing to give all the money I've paid for dog-fish livers in two years if that boy isn't on Cap'n Dock Vincent's track."

"Do you think so?" asked Mr. Watson, gathering fresh hope from the suggestion.

"I know it. I can't prove it, of course; but it's sort of burnt into me that he knows more about Bessie at this minute than any of the rest of us.

"I hope so."

"We found out yesterday" — this conversation was

on Wednesday — "that the Griffin went off on Monday night."

"But Levi was with me as late as nine o'clock."

"I don't know exactly how it's coming about; but you may mark my words, that Levi's on the track now."

Mr. Watson could only hope that Levi was in position to assist his daughter, if she were still living; but as it had been ascertained that the Griffin went out of the bay between four and five o'clock, while Levi had been with him as late as nine, he could not fully adopt the theory of the constable.

There was a great deal of interest manifested in the examination on Thursday forenoon. People were curious to know what would be done, and whether the bail would be forfeited. Levi could not appear, and people desired to know what would be said; so they assembled, to the utmost capacity of the room, in the squire's office, and twice as many more gathered around the door in the street. Mr. Watson was there, prepared with able counsel to argue for a postponement, and to pay every dollar of expense that had been or might be incurred. Mr. Fairfield

was there, convinced that Levi had run away, or
been drowned. Ruel Belcher was there, again im-
posing upon his brother-in-law the cruel necessity of
expending another twenty-five cents for " a slice from
the under side of the round." Mr. Gayles was not
there yet. He had gone to the post-office; but presently he appeared with a letter in his hand for Mr.
Watson, which he had observed through the glass
window of the office. He gave it to the merchant,
and entered into conversation with the counsel for
the defendant.

Squire Saunders said he was ready to proceed with
the business of the court, and would call up the case
of Levi Fairfield, continued from last Thursday. Mr.
Gayles stated that the defendant was not present.

"I knowed he wouldn't be," interposed Mr. Fairfield. "That boy has run away, and I knowed he
would all the time. He's a bad boy; but I hope
them that trusted him won't lose nothin by it."

"Do you know where he is, Mr. Fairfield?" asked
the justice.

"Do I? No; I don't know nothin about him.

THE RETURN OF THE STARRY FLAG. Page 284.

He's hardly been near my house sence he stole the money."

Mr. Cleaves, who had been employed as counsel for Levi, rose to state the case, and ask for a further continuation for a few days. He was confident that the defendant would appear in due time, and that he had no intention to evade the operation of the law.

" Merciful Heaven!" exclaimed Mr. Watson, suddenly rising from his chair with the letter he had just received in his hand, and his whole frame quivering with emotion.

" Have you any intelligence from the defendant?" asked Squire Saunders.

"No, sir; but I have from my daughter."

But then, as he thought of the condition of secrecy imposed upon him by Dock Vincent, he hastily folded up the letter, and thrust it into his pocket.

The letter was that which Dock Vincent had written on board the Griffin, and mailed at Rockland. What was twenty or fifty thousand dollars to the devoted father compared with the loss of his daughter? He was ready to give all the wretch asked to reclaim her.

24 *

"Where is she?" demanded the justice; and those in the room forgot all about Levi, for the moment, in their absorbing interest in the fate of Bessie.

"She is alive, and says she is well. Beyond this I am not permitted to say," replied Mr. Watson, as he moved towards the door, intent upon raising the money and hastening to the place indicated in the letter for the recovery of his daughter.

He found he could not go to Boston till three o'clock in the afternoon, and as his name and credit were good enough in Rockport to enable him to raise the required sum there, he determined to borrow the money, and proceed with his wife to Bangor. The Cape Ann *millionnaire*, one of Levi's bail, was present. He was the president of the bank, and promptly offered to supply the funds, though he was rather curious to know to what use the money was to be applied. But Mr. Watson kept his own counsel, fearful that Dock, if betrayed, would wreak his vengeance on his darling child. As nothing could be done, the merchant decided to remain at the office until Levi's case was disposed of for that day.

Squire Cleaves continued his remarks, urging his

reasons for a postponement of the examination. While he was thus engaged, a man, with more enthusiasm than discretion, rushed into the room.

"The Starry Flag is coming!" shouted he, at the top of his lungs.

"Where is she?" asked Mr. Gayles.

"She passed Halibut Point half an hour ago, and is headed towards Old Pier now."

"Is Levi in her?" continued Mr. Gayles.

"Yes, sir; and there is a girl with him."

"A girl!"

"A girl about a dozen years old, and we all reckon it's the one that was lost," replied the messenger. "I've been looking at 'em through my glass."

The court adjourned without any formalities whatever, and everybody rushed down to Old Pier, including the justice, the attorneys, the president of the bank, ministers, deacons, and laymen. Mr. Babson, who was at the justice's room, hastened to his house as fast as his fat legs would carry him, to inform Mrs. Watson that The Starry Flag was in sight, with a girl on board who was supposed to be Bessie. The anxious mother joined the crowd of people that flocked down to Old Pier, which now seemed to have half the population of the town gathered upon it.

The report was correct: The Starry Flag was coming, and by the time Mrs. Watson reached the wharf, and the crowd had opened for her so that she could join her husband on the edge of the pier, the boat was within hailing distance. Levi sat at the helm, his bosom bounding with emotions such as he had never experienced before. Bessie sat opposite to him, even more agitated than he. She recognized her father and mother on the wharf, and waved her handkerchief to them.

"It is she! It is she!" exclaimed the delighted father; and a thrill of joy flew through the hearts of the multitude.

A deafening cheer rose on the air, when it was certain that the girl was Bessie. Men swung their hats, and women their handkerchiefs, and the wave of rapture in the hearts of the multitude was mightier than the swell of the sea beneath them.

Levi waved his hat as he ran The Starry Flag into the dock, the proudest and the happiest fellow that ever handled a tiller or manned a halyard.

CHAPTER XXV.

THE RESULT OF THE EXAMINATION.

CHEER after cheer rent the air from the multitude on the pier as The Starry Flag entered
the dock, and sweeping round in a graceful circle,
came up to the stone steps where Mr. Gayles leaped
on board.

"How are you, Levi?" exclaimed the constable,
grasping the hand of the young fisherman.

"O, I'm all right," replied the blushing skipper of
The Starry Flag.

"And Miss Bessie — let me hand her up to her
father and mother," continued Mr. Gayles, taking the
little maiden by the arm. "We are so thankful you
are safe!"

"O, I am so happy!" replied Bessie, trembling
with emotion.

The cheers were continued by the excited crowd

as the kind-hearted officer conducted Bessie to the bow of the boat, and then up the steps, though she was clasped in her father's arms before she could reach the pier.

"My child!" cried Mrs. Watson, as her husband handed Bessie to her open arms.

It was a touching scene, and many others besides the father and mother wept for joy as Mrs. Watson pressed the lost one to her bosom, and thanked the good Father, from the deepest depths of her heart, for restoring her child. While these events were transpiring on the wharf, Levi let go his halyards, and then quietly seated himself at the stern of the boat, where he had sat most of the time for nearly three days. His eyes were deeply sunk in his head, and he was pale and haggard. He had slept but six hours during the whole cruise, and was worn out with watching, care, and anxiety. His mission seemed to be ended, and now he was hardly able to hold up his head.

"Three cheers for Levi Fairfield!" shouted the enthusiastic Cape Ann *millionnaire* on the pier.

The cheers were given with a hearty good will

as Bessie was handed into a carryall which one of the crowd pressed upon the parents.

"Where is Levi?" asked Mr. Watson, who, for the moment, had forgotten the brave deliverer of his daughter as the torrent of parental emotions flowed.

"He is in the boat," replied Mr. Gayles, rushing down the steps again to the Flag. "Come, Levi, you are wanted on shore," he added.

"I'm tired, Mr. Gayles," replied Levi; "and I guess I'll stay here till some of the folks have gone off."

"No; Mr. Watson wants to see you, and, besides, the court is waiting for you."

"I thought the court was down here," added Levi, with a faint smile. "I see Squire Saunders and others on the wharf. I'll stow my jib and mainsail, and go with you in a minute."

"We want to hear your story. You must have had a hard time of it, for it blew like sixty here last night."

"It blew some where I was."

Levi was not permitted to secure his sails, for

that office was taken from him by some fishermen,
and Mr. Gayles conducted him to the vehicle in
which Mrs. Watson and Bessie were seated. The
happy father grasped his hand as he approached,
and hurried him into the carryall, in which he
seated himself and drove off towards Mr. Babson's
house.

It had already been ascertained, from Bessie's
brief statement, that The Starry Flag had actually
sailed three hundred miles over the open ocean,
and had been to the mouth of the Penobscot.
Some of the crowd lingered to gaze upon her, and
express their admiration of her good behavior, and
the skill and daring of the youth who had piloted
her through the night, and the darkness, and the
storm, on her errand of mercy. The boat was
entitled to a portion of the credit, and she was
warmly praised. Mr. Hatch was almost as proud
and happy as though he had been on the cruise,
for he had built the boat, and she was a credit to
his skill.

"Don't tell me Levi stole that money, after this,"
said he, when the boat had been duly commended,

as the people walked back to the office of Squire
Saunders to hear the rest of the examination.

Mr. Watson drove up the street, and the carriage
was followed by a portion of the crowd, anxious
to learn the particulars of the cruise of The Starry
Flag.

"I don't know what would have become of me,
father, if it hadn't been for Levi," said Bessie.

"Some of the people supposed Levi had run
away; but Mr. Gayles was quite sure that he would
return."

"Uncle Nathan thought I had run away, I suppose," added Levi, rather dryly.

"He was sure of it."

"Poor child! What a hard time you have had!"
said Mrs. Watson, as she drew Bessie close to
her side.

"Indeed, I have not, mother," replied the little
wanderer; "at least not since I left Dock Vincent's
vessel."

"But you have been in an open boat all the
time."

"I slept in the little cabin all night, and didn't

wake up once, though Levi told me this morning he had had a gale of wind."

"You must have had a hard time of it, Levi," added Mr. Watson.

"Well, I am rather tired; but I shall be as good as new after I have made up my sleep."

The vehicle stopped at Mr. Babson's house, and the party went in. Mr. Gayles and others soon arrived. Between Bessie and Levi the story of the cruise was soon told. Mrs. Watson wept afresh as she listened to the perils through which her darling daughter had passed; and both father and mother wanted to hug Levi in their admiration for his noble daring, his skill, energy, and reso-lution.

"We must go to Squire Saunders's office now, Levi, if you feel able," interposed Mr. Gayles, when the story was finished.

"Not till he has had some breakfast," said Mrs. Babson, decidedly. "The poor fellow has been up all night, and I suppose he hasn't had even a cup of coffee to-day."

"The court is waiting."

"Let it wait," added Mrs. Babson. "If Squire Saunders can't stop for the poor boy to drink a cup of coffee, he isn't fit to be a judge."

The breakfast was all ready, and the wanderers sat down at the hospitable board. Mr. Gayles went to the magistrate's office, which was crowded with people, and told them the story to which he had just listened. They were all willing to wait for Levi as long as he wished ; and when he arrived with Mr. Watson, every man in the room insisted upon taking him by the hand — every one except Mr. Fairfield.

Uncle Nathan felt cheap. He would have sold himself out for sixpence. Levi was a lion, a hero. People would mob the justice if he attempted to bind him over for trial. The case was lost, so far as injuring Levi was concerned, and the guardian was even prepared to follow the popular current ; it was hardly safe for him to do otherwise, for the people might take it into their heads to pull his old buildings down if he persisted in persecuting his ward. But Mr. Fairfield realized that he had made two hundred and fifty dollars. Levi had

stolen the money, — he still believed this to be
the truth, — and he had obtained it. He had paid
it away, the money had gone to Boston, and there
was no longer any danger that it would be found
upon his person or his premises.

The case was opened again. The witnesses testi-
fied as before; but Dock Vincent was not present,
and Mr. Fairfield did not venture to repeat his
belief that Levi had stolen the money. Mr. Hatch,
as before, said he had received the bills for the
boat, but could not state positively that the bills
identified by Ruel Belcher were the ones paid to
him. Mr. Watson was called, and swore that he
had given two hundred and fifty dollars to Levi,
which the boy persisted in regarding as a loan.

"Could you identify the bills you paid to Levi
Fairfield?" asked Squire Cleaves, who acted as counsel for the defendant.

"I could," replied Mr. Watson, taking a memo-
randum book from his pocket. "It is my custom
to note down the number and description of all
bank bills larger than twenties which come into my
possession."

25 *

"Will you be kind enough to look at these bills ? " added Squire Cleaves, handing him three bank notes.

Mr. Watson took the bills, and compared their description with the memorandums before him.

"They are the bills I paid to Levi Fairfield," said he. "I checked them off of my book after I entered the train that morning."

"You are entirely sure ? "

"It is impossible that I should be mistaken."

"That will do; step down, if you please. Mr. Gayles, call Captain Treadwell."

The witness indicated was conducted to the table from an adjoining room. The crowd opened for him ; and when he appeared, Mr. Fairfield turned pale and trembled in every joint of his frame. The captain was sworn, and took the stand.

"Captain Treadwell, do you know these bills ? " continued Squire Cleaves.

"I do," replied the witness, after deliberately examining them.

".State what you know about them."

"They were paid to me by Mr. Fairfield. He

lent me five hundred dollars yesterday, and **these**
bills were part of the money."

"'Tain't so!" interrupted the miserable guardian
of Levi.

"Silence!" said the justice.

"I tell you I've had them bills for more'n two
months, and I didn't steal 'em nuther," persisted Mr.
Fairfield, desperately.

"Silence, sir! or I'll commit you for contempt,"
added Squire Saunders.

Mr. Fairfield "subsided," but the cold sweat stood
on his forehead, and his heart was almost in his
mouth.

"Go on, Captain Treadwell," said the counsel for
the defendant.

"Before Mr. Fairfield was out of sight, Mr. Gayles
came up, and wanted to see the money paid to me.
I showed it to him."

Mr. Gayles looked at Levi, and Levi looked at
Mr. Gayles. Both of them smiled. The constable
had kept one eye on the guardian all the time,
and when he went to Gloucester, had followed and
watched him. Mr. Fairfield had "reckoned without

his host," as bad men are apt to do. Levi's absence
had given him confidence to dispose of the bills;
and while the ward had served Bessie by his mission
to the Penobscot, he had served himself.

"It seems to me this is a clear case," said Squire
Cleaves, after all the evidence, including the defendant's, had been heard. "Levi paid this money
to Mr. Hatch; and the young man testifies that
these bills, identified by Mr. Watson, are the identical ones with which he paid for the boat. These
same bills are now paid by Mr. Fairfield to Captain
Treadwell. Where did Mr. Fairfield get them?
Of course, when Mr. Hatch permitted him to look
at them, he substituted the stolen bills for these;
and it follows, as the day follows the night, that
Mr. Fairfield stole them from his brother-in-law
himself."

"I didn't steal 'em — no sich thing!" shouted
Mr. Fairfield.

"Perhaps you will tell where you did get them,"
added Squire Cleaves.

"I found 'em in the chimbly," gasped the guardian, desperately.

" Can you inform the court how they came in the chimney ? "

" Levi hid 'em there," answered Mr. Fairfield, so confused and overborne by the unexpected revelations that his cunning forsook him, and he told what he believed to be the truth.

Mr. Fairfield was put upon the stand again, and actually told the whole truth — actually confessed that he had changed the bills.

" Why did you change them ? " asked the justice. " Did you wish to have your ward convicted ? "

" Sartinly not."

" Why, then ? "

" I'm that boy's guardeen, and I can't do nothin with him. He fit me t'other day like a wildcat; and — "

" What has that to do with it ? " demanded the justice, impatiently. " Tell the truth, or you shall be prosecuted for perjury."

" You're all down on me now; but I mean to tell the truth, as I allers did. Levi stole that money, and hid it in the chimbly. I knowed this.

Now, ef I hadn't changed the bills, the boy'd got off, and fooled all that money away on a boat. Ef the bills was found in the chimbly, I wanted it to look as ef Levi took the money he stole to buy the boat, and hid what Mr. Watson gin him in Ruel's wallet. As I fixed things, Ruel got his money back, and I got what Mr. Watson paid Levi — jist to keep for him, for I'm his guardeen."

It did not yet appear who had stolen the wallet. It lay between Levi and his uncle. There was not now a particle of evidence to prove that Levi was guilty, and he was accordingly discharged, much to the satisfaction of the spectators, who believed that Mr. Fairfield was the thief. Nothing could be proved; but it was supposed that the miser would be arrested in a day or two, after the lawyers had " compared notes."

Levi left the office, and was enthusiastically cheered by the crowd on the street. He went up to see Bessie and her mother again, promising to stay with Mr. Gayles over night.

Mr. Fairfield and Ruel Belcher went back to the old house, and spent the rest of the day in talking about the robbery. They could make nothing of it. Ruel would not admit that Levi stole his money, while his brother-in-law insisted upon his opinion. They became quite excited over the question, and the discussion was continued till a late hour in the evening, when Ruel retired.

"Massy sake! what's the matter?" exclaimed Mrs. Fairfield in the night, being awakened by a violent noise in Levi's chamber.

"Robbers — ain't it?" gasped the miser.

"I dunno; for massy sake, git up and find out."

"Seems as ef the rest of that chimbly's comin down."

Mr. Fairfield partially dressed himself, and went to. Levi's room. He was terribly frightened; but his money was as dear as his life, and he entered the room with a light in his hand.

On the hearth, with his head up the chimney, stood Ruel Belcher in his night-dress. His eyes were open, but he looked confused and stupid.

CHAPTER XXVI.

CONCLUSION.

CREATION, Ruel! 'What on airth are you doin in there?" demanded Mr. Fairfield, surprised rather than alarmed at the situation of his guest.

Ruel Belcher made no reply.

"What is it, Nathan? For pity's sake, tell me!" called Mrs. Fairfield, who had stationed herself at the foot of the stairs to listen.

"Come up here, wife."

"What's the matter?" continued Mrs. Fairfield, who had been partially assured by the voice and the tones of her husband.

"Sunthin ails Ruel," answered Mr. Fairfield, astonished that his brother-in-law did not speak.

"Goodness!" He ain't sick — is he?" said the wife, as she went up the stairs.

"There he is; he seems to be goin up chimbly."

"Goodness gracious! ef Ruel ain't at his old tricks!" ejaculated Mrs. Fairfield, holding up both hands in astonishment. "I thought he got cured of them long ago."

"Why, what ails him?"

"Don't you see, he gits up in his sleep? I don't know what he's doin in the chimbly."

"What shall I do? Shall I wake him up?"

"Jest kind o' coax him out if you can. They say it don't do sech folks no good to wake 'em up when they're at their tantrums."

Mr. Fairfield followed the advice of his wife; but Ruel was much more obstinate in his sleep than he was when awake, and was not inclined to be coaxed. He persisted in feeling of the bricks inside of the chimney, and appeared to be looking for something. His brother-in-law tried to make him stoop, and crawl out of the chimney; but he was obstinate, and did not seem to be conscious that he was not alone. Mr. Fairfield continued his efforts, which at last became so violent that he awoke the sleeper.

Ruel gave a "heavy start," a long gasp, and stared at his companion. In his operations he had

26

dislodged a brick, which had fortunately descended to the hearth without hitting him. He rubbed his eyes as he came to himself, and then yawned.

"What you doin in here, Ruel?" demanded Mr. Fairfield.

"I don't know. Where am I?" replied the sleep-walker.

"Stoop down, and git out; you were goin up chimbly, I s'pose."

Ruel obeyed, and bent his head enough to enable him to pass out into the chamber.

"Massy sake!" ejaculated his sister.

"What do you want? What are you doing here?" asked Ruel, apparently more astonished than any one else at the awkwardness of the situation.

"What are *you* doin, Ruel?" added Mrs. Fairfield.

"I'm not doing anything — at least, I don't know anything about it," continued Ruel, with a look of blank amazement.

"Well, git into bed again; you'll git your death o' cold, poking round with nothin on but your night clothes."

Ruel was quite tractable now; but it was found that his hands were covered with "crock," and after washing them he retired again.

"What was you doin in the chimbly, Ruel?" asked Mr. Fairfield.

"I don't know."

"You are at your old tricks again," added Mrs. Fairfield. "When you was a young man, you used to git up in your sleep a'most every night, and we used to be scared a'most to death for fear sunthin would happen to you. I know you got up one night and hunted all over the house for a half dollar you had lost. I s'pose you was worried about it."

"Can't you tell what you was a dreamin on?" asked Mr. Fairfield.

Ruel rubbed his eyes, and thought a moment.

"It comes to me now," said he. "I was dreaming of that wallet I lost. It seemed to me just as though I had put it somewhere, and was going to look for it."

"I vow, Ruel, you put that wallet in the chimbly yourself, jest where Nathan found it!" exclaimed his sister, a flood of light suddenly bursting in upon her.

"I shouldn't wonder; but I didn't know I got up in my sleep any of late years," replied Ruel, with a sheepish look, as he thought of the mischief which his involuntary act had caused.

"You ain't to blame, of course. I hain't seen much of you sence I was married, and I never thought of sech a thing as your gittin up in your sleep now days."

"I remember now that my hands were covered with crock in the morning after I slept with Levi; but I didn't think anything of it. I supposed I got it on somewhere round the stove," added Ruel.

"Yes, and I found the sheets smooched too; but Levi's allers into the dirt so deep that it didn't strike me as anything strange," said his sister.

"I'm very sorry for the trouble I've caused; but I didn't mean to do it."

"Of course you couldn't help it. One thing is sartin, now, that Levi didn't steal that money."

"I s'pose he didn't; but I guess it ain't best

to say anything about this matter," said Mr. Fairfield.

"Not say anything about it!" exclaimed Ruel, rising up in the bed.

"'Tain't best — is it!"

"I think it is; we'll tell the truth, at any rate."

Ruel was an honest man, and he was not willing that even a suspicion should any longer rest upon Levi while he had the means of exonerating him.

"I don't know how it'll work to tell on't," said Mr. Fairfield.

"I don't care how it works. No harm has been done to any one yet. You changed the bills in the hands of Mr. Hatch, Nathan. That was wrong."

"But I was just as sartin as I could be that. Levi stole that money."

"Well, why didn't you tell of it when you found it in the chimney?" demanded Ruel, indignantly.

"I was just as sartin that Levi hid it there. All I wanted was to keep the boy from foolin away his money."

Ruel was not willing to believe this. He was

satisfied that the miser intended to convict the boy of the crime, and he was determined that the whole truth should be told. The parties all went back to bed. In the morning Ruel went to Squire Saunders, full of mortification and regret, and narrated the scene we have described, deducing from the fact that his hands were covered with "crock" on the morning after the loss of his money the real truth, that he had hidden the wallet in the chimney himself. Mr. Watson, Mr. Gayles, and Levi were sent for, and the whole matter was carefully considered. While the party in the lawyer's office were thus occupied, Mr. Fairfield and his wife appeared, for the miser was unwilling that anything about him should be said behind his back.

Ruel, in his anxiety for the safety of his money, during his first visit, had dreamed about it, and being a sleep-walker, had risen from his bed under the influence of this anxiety, and placed the wallet where his brother-in-law had found it. After the second examination, he and Mr. Fairfield had conversed till a late hour at night about the guilt of Levi, and doubtless the excitement had followed him into his sleep; and again dreaming of his wallet, he had got up to search for it. This explanation, with the testimony of his sister in regard to his early sleep-walking habit, fully satisfied those present that the real truth had been reached at last. It cleared Levi of even the shadow of a suspicion.

It also relieved Mr. Fairfield of the guilt of stealing the wallet, but not of the fact that he had changed the bills; and it was in vain for him to plead that he had done so only to prevent Levi from "foolin away the money."

"Mr. Fairfield," said Squire Saunders, "you have proved that you are not a fit person to have the charge of a young man like Levi."

"Why not, — I'd like to know," demanded the miser.

"In the first place, you are not an honest man. You have done your best to convict the young man of a crime of which he was not guilty."

"I had good reason to believe he was guilty."

"You had no right to change the bills; and you are guilty of perjury and conspiracy. You have done enough to send you to the State Prison now."

" For pity's sake ! " ejaculated Mrs. Fairfield.

" I do not know that it is advisable to proceed against you; but it is certainly highly improper that you should continue to be the guardian of your nephew, or that his property should be longer intrusted to your keeping. Levi, do you wish to remain with your uncle ? " continued Squire Saunders, turning to the young fisherman.

" No, sir," replied he, decidedly.

" Then you may petition the Probate Court to remove your guardian and appoint another. Do you think of any person you would like to have ? "

" Yes, sir — Mr. Gayles."

" Very well; I will see that the proper papers are made out."

Levi had no malice against his uncle, for he had not vainly studied the words and contemplated the divine example of Him who said, " Love your enemies, bless them that curse you, do good to them that hate you, and pray for them which despitefully use you and persecute you." It was not necessary that he should live with his uncle, and be starved and buffeted in the future as he had been in the past; but it was necessary that no thought of evil or revenge should lurk in his heart.

Mr. Watson, Mr. Gayles, and others thought that Mr. Fairfield should be prosecuted for perjury in swearing that he did not change the bills, and for conspiracy in attempting to procure the conviction of his ward; but Levi pleaded for him, and begged that no steps might be taken.

"Now, Levi, you must dine with us to-day," said Mr. Watson. "Bessie is not satisfied when you are out of sight. And, Mr. Gayles, you must come too."

Bessie welcomed the young fisherman like a brother, and as the truest of friends. They talked over the cruise of The Starry Flag till dinner time, and Levi insisted that the excursion to Thatcher's Island should take place the next day.

"Mr. Gayles, you are to be Levi's guardian; I suppose it is a settled fact," said Mr. Watson, as the party seated themselves under the piazza, on the shady side of the house, after dinner.

"If I am I shall do the best I can for him," replied Mr. Gayles. "If it hadn't been for him,

I should not be here now, for he saved my life, even while I had a warrant for his arrest in my pocket."

"You have been a good friend to him, and he believes in you — to use his own expression. Yesterday I made arrangements to pay that wretch, Dock Vincent, twenty-two thousand dollars to restore Bessie to me. If Levi had not returned with her as he did, I should have been on my way to Bangor in the afternoon. The money was nothing; but it seems to me no more than right that I should do as much for Levi — honest, faithful, and brave — as I was willing to do for that miserable, cowardly scoundrel who carried off my child. As soon, therefore, as you are appointed the guardian of Levi, I shall pay over to you the sum of twenty-two thousand dollars, to be held in trust for him until he is twenty-one, when it shall be his own."

"No, sir!" protested Levi. "I don't want anything of that sort done. I don't do that kind of jobs for money."

Mr. Watson was determined to have his own way, and Levi, in spite of himself, was made a rich man.

At the next session of the Probate Court, Mr. Fairfield was removed, and Mr. Gayles appointed the guardian of Levi. The miser groaned when he was compelled to give up the property of his late ward. It was like taking out his teeth, especially as Mr. Gayles inquired very closely into every investment, and refused to pay some exorbitant bills for board and clothing. But the business was happily finished, and Levi was duly installed in his new home at Mr. Gayles's house.

Dock Vincent, when he found he could not overtake The Starry Flag, put back to a port in Maine, where he sold his vessel and paid off his men. It was several weeks before he ventured to appear on Cape Ann again; but even that time was too soon, for he was arrested, tried, and sentenced to the State Prison for a term long enough to give him ample opportunity for repentance and reformation.

Mr. Watson has paid over the twenty-two thousand dollars to Levi's guardian; Mr. Hatch has received the money for The Starry Flag; and the young fisherman is no longer obliged to catch dog-fish to obtain a comfortable living and a good edu. cation.

The excursion to Thatcher's Island came off as arranged, and the party had a splendid time; and, though Jenny and Estelle "made fun" at the expense of Levi and Bessie, the latter seemed to enjoy it quite as much as her companions.

Mr. Watson purposes to erect a summer residence at Rockport, for Bessie declares that she must go there every season as long as she lives. Last spring, Levi spent a fortnight in Boston; and he was dressed so nicely and looked so manly, besides being so brave, noble, and good, that Bessie was proud to go with him to the concerts and lectures; and withal, he invariably created quite a sensation when he was introduced. Knowing people declare that he will eventually possess all Mr. Watson's large property; for Bessie still thinks there is no young man like Levi, and takes the greatest delight in telling about THE STARRY FLAG, and THE YOUNG FISHERMAN OF CAPE ANN.

Lee and Shepard's Publications.

Play and Study Series for Boys and Girls. By
Mrs. Madeline Leslie. Four volumes. Illustrated. Uniform with Little Agnes Library for Girls. Neat box. Per volume, $1.50. Comprising: The Motherless Children; Play and Study; Howard and his Teacher; Jack, the Chimney Sweeper. These two popular series are issued in entirely new style, bound in rich fancy cloths, and put up in neat box.

Ned Nevins the Newsboy; or, Street Scenes in
Boston. By Rev. Henry Morgan, P. M. P. 16mo. Illustrated. $1.50.

Old Merry Rhymes for Young Merry Hearts.
Small 4to.- Boards. 25 cts.

Little Prudy Stories. By Sophie May. Now
complete. Six volumes. 24mo. Handsomely illustrated. In a neat box. Per volume, 75 cts. Comprising: Little Prudy; Little Prudy's Sister Susie; Little Prudy's Captain Horace; Little Prudy's Cousin Grace; Little Prudy's Story-Book; Little Prudy's Dotty Dimple.

Patriotism at Home; or, The Young Invincibles.
By I. H. Anderson, author of "Fred Freeland." With four illustrations, from original designs by Champney. One volume. 16mo. $1.50.

Rosy Diamond Story-Books. For Girls. A com-
panion set to Vacation Story-Books. Finely illustrated from designs by Billings and others. Six volumes. Bound in high-colored cloths. In neat box. Per volume, 80 cts. Comprising: The Great Rosy Diamond; Daisy, or the Fairy Spectacles; Violet, a Fairy Story; Minnie, or the Little Woman; The Angel Children; Little Blossom's Reward.

Vacation Story-Books. For Boys and Girls
Finely illustrated from designs by Hoppin and others. Six volumes. Square 16mo. In neat box. Per volume 80 cts. Comprising: Worth, not Wealth; Country Life; The Charm; Karl Keigler; Walter Seyton; Holidays at Chestnut Hill.

Sunnybank Stories. Twelve volumes. Compiled
by Rev. Asa Bullard, editor of the "Well-Spring." Profusely illustrated. 32mo. Bound in high colors, and put up in neat box. Per volume, 25 cts. Comprising: Uncle Henry's Stories; Dog Stories; Stories for Alice; My Teacher's Gem; The Scholar's Welcome; Going to School; Aunt Lizzie's Stories; Mother's Stories' Grandpa's Stories; The Good Scholar; The Lighthouse; Reward of Merit.
The same series is also divided into Sunnybank and Shady Dell Stories, of six volumes each. Orders should designate the number of volumes required.

Shady Dell Stories. Six volumes. Compiled by
Rev. Asa Bullard, editor of the "Well-Spring." Profusely illustrated. 32mo. Bound in high colors, and put up in a neat box (to match the Sunnybank Stories). Per volume, 25 cts. Comprising: My Teacher's Gem; The Scholar's Welcome; Going to School; The Good Scholar; The Lighthouse; Reward of Merit.

Sunnybank Stories. Six volumes. Compiled by
Rev. Asa Bullard, editor of the "Well-Spring." Profusely illustrated. 32mo. Bound in high colors and put up in a neat box. Per volume, 25 cts. Comprising: Uncle Henry's Stories; Dog Stories; Stories for Alice; Aunt Lizzie's Stories; Mother's Stories; Grandpa's Stories.

Willis the Pilot; or, Sequel to the Swiss Family
Robinson. With numerous illustrations. 16mo. $1.50.

Arabian Nights' Entertainments. 12mo. Muslin.
With eight full-page illustrations. (The popular edition formerly published by Phillips, Sampson & Co.) $1.75.

Amateur Dramas for Parlor Theatricals, Evening
Entertainments, and School Exhibitions. By Geo. M. Baker. Illus. 16mo. $1.50.

Glimpses of History. By George M. Towle.
One volume. 16mo. Bevelled boards. $1.50.

The Heavenly Father: Lectures on Modern Athe-
ism. By Ernest Naville, late Professor of Philosophy in the University of Geneva. Translated from the French, by Henry Downton, M. A. Published in a handsome 16mo volume. $1.75.

Home Life: What it Is, and What it Needs. By
Rev. J. F. W. Ware. 16mo. Cloth, red edges, bevelled sides. $1.25.

Herman; or Young Knighthood. By E. Foxton.
Two volumes. 12mo. $3.50.

Historical Sketch of the Old Sixth Regiment of
Massachusetts Volunteers, during its three campaigns in 1861, 1862, 1863, and 1864; containing the History of the several Companies previous to 1861, and the name and military record of each man connected with the regiment during the war. By John W. Hanson, Chaplain. Illustrated by photographs. 12mo. $2.50.

Hospital Life in the Army of the Potomac. By
William Howell Reed. 16mo. $1.25.

The Irish Ninth in Bivouac and Battle. By M. H.
Macnamara, late Captain in the Ninth Massachusetts Regiment. Illustrated. 12mo. Cloth. Sold by subscription. $2.00.

In Trust; or Dr. Bertrand's Household. By Miss
Douglas. One volume. 12mo. $1.50.

Stephen Dane. By Miss Douglas, author of "In
Trust." $1.50.

Some of the Thoughts of Joseph Joubert. With
a Biographical Notice. By G. H. Calvert. 16mo. Tinted paper. Cloth, bvld. $1.50.

Life of Jesus. According to his Original Biog-
raphers. By Edmund Kirke. 16mo. $1.50.

Lincolniana. In one volume, small quarto. pp.
viii. and 344. (Only 250 copies printed.) $6.00.

The Little Helper. A Memoir of Florence Annie
Caswell. By Lavina S. Goodwin. (In press.)

The Life and Works of Gotthold Ephraim Lessing.
Translated from the German of Adolf Starr, by E. P. Evans, Ph. D., Michigan University. Two volumes, crown octavo. $5.00.

Little Brother, and other Stories. By Fitz Hugh
Ludlow. $1.50.

Manual of the Evidences of Christianity. For
Classes and Private Reading. By Rev. S. G. Bulfinch, D. D. 12mo. $1.25.

Martyria; or, Andersonville Prison. By Lieu-
tenant-Colonel A. C. Hamlin, late Medical Inspector in the Army. Illustrated with maps and cuts. One volume. 12mo. $2.00.

Memoir of Timothy Gilbert. By Rev. J. D. Ful-
ton, of Tremont Temple, Boston. With Portrait. One volume. 12mo. $1.50

Neighbors' Wives. By J. T. Trowbridge. 12mo.
Cloth. $1 50.

Twice Taken. A Tale of the Maritime British
Provinces. By Charles W. Hall. 12mo. $1.75.

Ten Months in Brazil. By Captain John Codman
("Ringbolt"). In press.

Talks on Women's Topics. By Jennie June. One
volume. 12mo. Gilt Tops. $1.75.

A Thousand a Year. By Mrs. E. M. Bruce. One
volume. 16mo. $1.25.

Three Years in the Army of the Potomac. By
Captain Henry N. Blake, Eleventh Mass. Volunteers. One vol. 12mo. $1.50.

Thomas à Becket. A Tragedy, and other Poems.
By G. H. Hollister. 16mo. $1.75.

A View at the Foundations; or, First Causes of
Character. By Rev. W. M. Fernald. 12mo. Cloth. $1.00.

The White Mountain Guide-Book. By Samuel C.
Eastman. $1.50.

Why Not? A Book for every Woman. By Prof.
H. R. Storer, M. D. 16mo. Cloth, $1.00; paper, 50 cts.

Dillaway's Latin Classics. Cicero de Senectute,
et de Amicitia; Cicero de Officiis; Cicero de Oratore — two volumes; Cicero Tus-
culanæ Quæstiones — two volumes; Cicero de Natura de Orum — two volumes;
Tacitus Germania et Agricola; Terence; Quintilian; Plautus. Per vol , $1.00.

French Written as Pronounced; a Manual of
French Pronunciation, with Extracts from the French Classics, written in Pho-
netic Characters. By Adrien Feline. Revised, with additions by Wm. Watson,
Ph. D. One volume. 16mo. $1.25.

First Lessons in Reading; a New Method of
Teaching the Reading of English, by which the ear is trained to discriminate the
elementary sounds of words, and the eye to recognize the signs used for these
sounds in the established Orthography. By Richard Soule, editor of Worcester's
Quarto Dictionary, and William A. Wheeler, editor of Webster's Quarto Dictionary.
16mo. Boards. 35 cts. Sequel to the above. (In preparation).

Charts, designed to accompany the "First Lessons
in Reading (on a new method)," and a Sequel to the same. By Richard Soule
and William A. Wheeler. Price of the series (six charts), mounted on stiff bind-
ers' board, $2.50; any two thus mounted, $1.00; single Charts (not mounted), 40c
These last will be sent by mail to any address, on receipt of the price; they will
be found very convenient for posting upon the walls of the school-room.

A Manual of English Pronunciation and Spelling;
containing a full Alphabetical Vocabulary of the Language, with a preliminary
exposition of the English Orthoepy and Orthography, and designed as a work of
reference for general use, and as a Text-Book in schools. By Richard Soule, Jr.,
A. M., and Wm. A. Wheeler, A. M. A convenient Manual for consultation. $2.00.

Kindergarten Spelling Book. Part First. By
Ella Little. 16mo. Boards. 25 cts.

The Phonic Primer and Primary Reader. By
Rev. J. C. Zachos. 12mo. Boards. 35 cts.

A Trip to the Azores, or Western Islands. By
L. Borges De F. Henriques. 16mo. $1.50.

Bacon's Essays. With Annotations by Archbishop
Whately. In press; new edition. This edition will contain a Preface, Notes, and
Glossarial Index, by F. F. Heard, Esq., of the Boston Bar. It will be printed in
the very best style, by Messrs. J. Wilson & Son, of Cambridge, and will undoubtedly be the finest edition ever published in this country.

The Blade and the Ear. Thoughts for a Young
Man. By Rev. A. B. Muzzey. 16mo. Red edges, bvld sides, $1.50; plain. $1.25.

The College, the Market, and the Court; or,
Woman s Relation to Education, Employment, and Citizenship. By Mrs. Caro-
line H. Dall. $2.50.

Darryll Gap · or, Whether it Paid. A novel. By
Miss Virginia F. Townsend. One volume. 12mo. pp. 456. $1.75.

Dearborn's American Text-Book of Letters; with
a Diagram of the Capital Script Alphabet. By N. S. Dearborn. Oblong. $1.50.

Diary, from March 4, 1861, to November 13, 1862.
By Adam Gurowski. $1.75.

Dissertations and Discussions. By John Stuart
Mill. Three volumes. 12mo. Cloth. $6.75.

The Examination of the Philosophy of Sir William
Hamilton. By John Stuart Mill. Two volumes. 12mo. Cloth. Per vol., $2.25.

The Positive Philosophy of Auguste Comte. By
John Stuart Mill. One volume. 12mo. Cloth. $1.25.

Elements of Heraldry; containing an Explanation
of the Principles of the Science, and a Glossary of the Technical Terms employed.
With an Essay upon the use of Coat-Armor in the United States. By William H.
Whitmore. 8vo. Cloth. $6.00.

Essays: Philosophical and Theological. By James
Martineau. Crown octavo. Tinted paper. $2.50.

Facts about Peat as an Article of Fuel. By T. H.
Leavitt. 12mo. $1.75.

First · Historical Transformations of Christianity.
By A. Coquerel. Translated by Prof. E. P. Evans, of Michigan University. 12mo.
$1.25.

First Years in Europe. By G. H. Calvert, author
of " Scenes and Thoughts in Europe," " The Gentleman," etc. 1 vol. 12mo. $1.75

The Gold-Hunter's Adventures; or, Life in Aus-
tralia. By W. H. Thomes, a Returned Australian. Illust. by Champney. $2.00.

The Bushrangers: A Yankee's Adventures during
his second visit to Australia. By W. H. Thomes, author of the " Gold-Hunter's
Adventures"; or, Life in Australia." One vol. 12mo. Handsomely illust. $2.00

God in his Providence. By Rev. W. M. Fernald.
12mo. Cloth. $1.50.

Arabian Nights. 16mo. Illustrated. $1.50.

The Adventures of a German Toy. A charming
story for children. By Miss E. P. Channing. With three illustrations. 75 cts.

Crusoe Library. An attractive series for Young
and Old. Six volumes, illustrated. In neat box. Per volume, $1.50. Comprising: Robinson Crusoe; Arabian Nights; Arctic Crusoe; Young Crusoe; Prairie
Crusoe; Will is the Pilot.

Robinson Crusoe. 16mo. Illustrated. $1.50.

The Young Crusoe. A book for Boys. 16mo.
Illustrated. $1.50.

The Prairie Crusoe; or, Adventures in the Far
West. A book for Boys. 16mo. Illustrated. $1.50.

The Arctic Crusoe: A Tale of the Polar Seas.
Finely illustrated. 16mo. $1.50.

Eminent Statesmen. The Young American's Li-
brary of Eminent Statesmen. Uniform with the Young American's Library of
Famous Generals. Six volumes, handsomely illustrated, in neat box. Per vol.,
$1.25. Comprising: Life of Benjamin Franklin; Life of Daniel Webster; The
Yankee Tea Party; Life of William Penn; Life of Henry Clay; Old Bell of
Independence.

Famous Generals. The Young American's Li-
brary of Famous Generals. A useful and attractive series of books fo. Boys.
Six volumes, handsomely illustrated, in neat box. Per volume, $1.25. Compris-
ing: Life of General Washington; Life of General Taylor; Life of General Jack-
son; Life of General Lafayette; Life of General Marion; Life of Napoleon
Bonaparte.

Fireside Picture Books. With many comical illus-
trations. Stiff paper covers, in assorted dozen; per dozen, $1.80. Stiff paper
covers, in assorted dozen, colored; per dozen, $3.00. Comprising: Precocious
Piggy; Robber Kitten; Nine Lives of a Cat; Picture Alphabet; Little Man and
his Little Gun; Fireside Picture Alphabet.

Glen Morris Stories for Boys and Girls. By
Frances Forrester. Five volumes, 16mo. Each volume complete in itself, and
beautifully illustrated with fine engravings. Per volume, $1.25. Comprising:
Guy Carlton; Dick Duncan; Jessie Carlton; Walter Sherwood; Kate Carlton.

Kitty Barton. By Hester Gray. A simple Story
for Children. With one illustration. 32mo. 60 cts.

The Little Wrinkled Old Man. A Christmas
Extravaganza, and other Trifles. By Mrs. Elizabeth A. Thurston. Illust. 75c.

Minnie and her Pets. By Mrs. Madeline Leslie.
Elegantly illustrated. Six volumes. Small 4to. Bound in high-colored cloth,
and put up in neat box. Per volume, 75 cts. Comprising: Minnie's Pet Parrot;
Minnie's Pet Cat; Minnie's Pet Dog; Minnie's Pet Pony; Minnie's Pet Lamb;
Minnie's Pet Monkey.

Little Agnes' Library for Girls. By Mrs. Madeline
Leslie. Four volumes, in neat box; each volume elegantly illustrated, and en-
tirely distinct from the rest. Per volume, $1.50. Comprising: Little Agnes;
Trying to be Useful; I'll Try; Art and Artlessness.

The Negro in the American Rebellion ; his Hero-
om and his Fidelity. By William Wells Brown. Sold by subscription. $2.00.

Our Convicts. Two volumes in one. By Miss
Mary Carpenter. pp. 293 and 380. Octavo. $4.50.

On the Border. By Edmund Kirke. $1.75.

Orographic Geology ; or, The Origin and Struc-
ture of Mountains. By. George L. Vose, Civil Engineer. 8vo. Cloth. $3.00.

Practical and Scientific Fruit Culture. By Charles
R. Baker, Dorchester Nurseries. One volume. 8vo. Cloth. $4.00.

Robinson Crusoe. 12mo. Muslin gilt. With
sixteen full-page illustrations. (The edition formerly published by Phillips, Sampson & Company.) $1.75.

Redeemer and Redeemed ; an Investigation of the
Atonement and of Eternal Judgment. By the Rev. Charles Beecher, Pastor of
the Congregational Church, Georgetown, Mass. $1.75.

Reason in Religion. · By Rev. F. H. Hedge, D. D.
One volume. Crown octavo. $2.00.

Reid's (Captain Mayne) Books. Each volume
handsomely illustrated. Sold in sets or separate. Per volume, $1.75. The Wild
Huntress, or Love in the Wilderness; The Wood-Rangers, or The Trappers of
Sonora ; Wild Life, or Adventures on the Frontier; Hunter's Feast, or Conversa-
tions around the Camp-Fire; The Scalp-Hunters, or Adventures among the
Trappers; The White Chief, a Legend of Northern Mexico; The Rifle-Rangers,
or Adventures in Southern Mexico; The War Trail, or The Hunt of the Wild
Horse; The Quadroon, or a Lover's Adventures in Louisiana; Osceola, the Sem-
inole, or the Red Fawn of the Flower Land; The Rangers and Regulators of the
Tahama, or Life among the Lawless; The Maroon, or Planter Life in Jamaica ;
The Tiger-Hunter, or a Hero in spite of himself; Lost Leonore.

Religious Duty. By Frances Power Cobbe. 12mo.
Cloth, bevelled sides. $1.75.

Studies, New and Old, of Ethical and Social Sub-
jects. By Frances Power Cobbe. Crown 8vo. $3.00. Contents: Christian
Ethics and the Ethics of Christ: Self-Development and Self-Abnegation ; The
Sacred Books of the Zoroastrians; The Philosophy of the Poor Laws; The Rights
of Man and the Claims of Brutes; The Morals of Literature; The Hierarchy of
Art ; Decemnovenarianism ; Hades.

Shakings. Etchings from the Naval Academy.
By a Member of the Class of '67. $5.00.

"Swingin' Round the Cirkle." A new volume,
by Petroleum V. Nasby; containing his late humorous contributions to our politi
cal history, with new matter never before published. Appropriately illustrated
by T. Nast. 12mo. $1.50.

Stories and Sketches. By our best Authors.
$1.50.

Serpents in the Doves' Nest. By John Todd, D. D.
Paper 15 cts.; cloth, 50 cts.

The Soldier's Story of his Captivity at Anderson-
ville, Belle Isle, and other Re el Prisons. By Warren Lee Goss, of the Second
Massachusetts Heavy Artillery. Illustrated by Thomas Nast. 12mo. (Sold by
subscription.) $2.00.

www.ingramcontent.com/pod-product-compliance
Lightning Source LLC
Chambersburg PA
CBHW020943030726
47496CB00005B/1323